Reason Why

Book Five • Island Series

Tudor Robins

Other Books by Tudor Robins:

Island Series:
Six-Month Horse (Prequel)
Wednesday Riders (Book Two)
Join Up (Book Three)
Faults (Book Four)
Reason Why (Book Five)

Stonegate Series:
Objects in Mirror (Book One)
After Lucas (Book Two)
Throw Your Heart Over (Book Three)

Perryside Series:
Moving North (Book One)

Mystery Stables:
Stolen Saddles (Book One)

Stand-Alones:
Meant to Be (Young Adult)
Before & After (Women's Fiction)
In Search Of (Small-Town Romance)

Note to readers

The Island short story *Merry and Bright* precedes this novel and fills in some of the details about how Meg and Jared got to where they are as *Reason Why* opens.

If you haven't already read it, please feel free to download your copy from **https://tinyurl.com/MegJared** .

You can also use this QR code to take you directly to the download page:

Thank you for reading!

Meg

IF THIS HORSE had run like this on the track, maybe he'd still be there.

Everything about this horse captivates her. His name – possibly her all-time favourite – He's Got Hops. The fascinating white lacing etched through his rich chestnut coat – for the moment his saddle covers it, but the vet said it'll spread as he ages. Mostly, though, she loves his personality. He's by far the biggest horse in her string – a leggy 17.2hh – but he loves to cuddle. Any time she's within reach he'll rest his chin on her shoulder, or even the top of her head. Of course she loves boss-mare Salem, and Austen's slightly scatterbrained Mac, but Hops is just so endearing.

Also, despite being sold off the track with no winnings to his name, full of run.

Meg's playing a game with herself. Be as quiet on his back as possible. Stay as balanced as she can. Don't do anything to interfere with his gallop and see how long he chooses to keep going.

They've already covered more than two kilometres, first on the grassy shoulder alongside the gravel road, then swinging onto a wide track cutting across fields. He didn't slow when they made that initial transition, and he didn't hesitate as the path cut through a woodlot.

If anything, his pace felt faster to her then, with the trees whipping by on either side. He bursts back into the open field without slackening his tempo. A deer grazing off to the side whips her head up, but beyond the flick of an ear, Hops doesn't even acknowledge her.

This horse is the real deal.

This horse has endurance beyond her wildest dreams.

This horse is bombproof.

Talk about forgetting all her problems on the back of a horse – Meg isn't thinking about how she doesn't have a dress for her wedding – which is tomorrow. She's not thinking about how her mother's here, and how she really can't find out Meg doesn't have a dress.

Meg's hardly thinking at all. On this late-summer day, when the humidity normally confined to the mainland has found them on the island, she's enjoying the cooling wind in her face, the dull thud of hoofbeats on the springy surface of the trail, and the feeling of being completely in sync with the rhythm of this horse.

When she does think, it's about how this horse can go anywhere, do anything. How with his run, and his attitude, he could be the best eventer she's ever ridden.

Not that she gets to keep him. But that doesn't matter, because right now, today, she's the one riding him.

They enter the second woodlot, flying, with the gelding's breath still coming easily and the skin of his neck under her hand just slightly warm. She laughs out loud. He's going to gallop all the way to the ferry.

He goes from four-beat to no beat in three strides.

Meg goes from what she thought was perfectly balanced to halfway-up-his-neck in the blink of an eye.

The blink of a fox's eye.

Because that's what's caused all this. A fox, sitting on top of a log fallen across the trail.

The fox blinks again. His black-speckled, white-tipped tail is draped across his feet.

He yawns.

Hops reels backward.

"Oh no you don't." Meg's wrestled her way back into the saddle. As soon as she applies leg to stop the reverse motion, she feels the subtle shift in the horse's weight. He's loading his hindquarters, freeing his front end.

She can't let him go up.

The horse's stunning looks, sweeping stride, and scopey free jumping, were his ticket into a show jumping barn outside Kingston. A rearing incident that left his rider on the ground with a broken arm was his ticket to her.

Given the severe bit, restrictive noseband, and cranked-down martingale the horse was wearing the day Meg saw him, she wasn't too worried – tied down like that she would have wanted to rear, too.

He hasn't gone up once while she's had him, and there's no way she's letting him start now.

She backs up her leg with her seat and loops the rein.

It's all about respect. She understands his fear. She's not going to try to force him to march right up to the fox. But she's also not letting him run away – not on four legs, and not on two.

The step he takes forward is more out of confusion than willingness, but she praises it – "good boy," – and keeps her eyes forward, fixed on a tree in the woods beside the fox-adorned log.

Hops takes a second step. "Yes," she scratches his withers.

He sighs and arches his neck, picking up a light contact with her hand and keeps moving.

"All I want is a figure eight in front of the log," she tells him.

It's jerky. It's uneven. He rushes on the curve away from the fox, and stilts his steps on the diagonal heading back.

He does it though. He doesn't rear.

As much as Meg would prefer they hadn't come to a screeching halt, and that they were still on the way to the ferry, she has to admit this is a good test.

If he won't leave the ground under these circumstances, she thinks it's fair to say he's not a rearer.

The figure eights are much smoother now and she moves each one incrementally closer to the log.

The watching fox is less than impressed. He yawns again, which shoots a frisson of tension through the gelding.

In the whisker of time that Meg and Hops are angled away from him, the fox disappears. It happens in silence and with no telltale movement of vegetation left behind. It's as though he melted into the brush.

Hops sweeps his ears forward and a quiver runs through his body – she can feel it under her legs and traveling up the reins to her hands – telling her he wants to fling himself over the log. *"No fox!"* Meg imagines him saying. *"Let's go!"*

"Hey. You don't just get your way the second you decide you want to go."

She rides him forward through another complete figure eight but the truth is, she wants to go, too. She wants to be at the dock when the ferry glides in.

So, as they cross the centre of the figure eight, instead of curving the horse back along the outline they've been following, she rides him straight ahead and into a forward trot. Two strides carry them to the base of the log and he jumps it twice as big as he needs to, landing in a forward canter, asking her if he can move up to a hand gallop.

La-cey-Fitch, La-cey-Fitch ... the syllables of their names run through Meg's head in time with the three-beat rhythm of Hop's stride.

They'll be on the ferry right now. Driving off in just a few minutes.

She wants to be there to wave at Lacey. To welcome her home.

Of course she's excited to see her – as one of Meg's longest friends on the island, and as Jared's cousin, Lacey was the first person Meg asked to be a bridesmaid.

There's also been something not-quite-right about Lacey lately. Lacey's famous for losing the spelling bee finals in grade eight because she spelled as quickly as she speaks – too fast for the judges to hear all the letters. She's known for taking glass-half-full to a whole new level, riding with a cast on her right arm for six weeks and telling Meg, "It turned out to be a good thing I broke my right arm, because my left one was too weak before."

But the last few times they've talked, Lacey's been quiet. Not an indecipherable sentence, or a fit of giggles to be heard.

When they spoke a few days ago, just as Lacey and Fitch were packing up for the big drive from Halifax, Meg asked, "How long can you stay?"

There was a long pause. "I don't know."

"Do you still have your job at the university stables?"

"Hmm? Oh, yeah. The plan is for me to take ten days off."

"The plan? Is that not definite?"

A sigh traveled to Meg's ear. "You know, I really don't want to talk about it right now. I just can't wait to get home, and see everyone – and Salem – and, of course, go to your wedding."

"Sure," Meg said, "That's fine. We'll go for a bunch of hacks while you're home and we can catch up then."

Lacey gave a tiny giggle then. "Um, since I'm coming back for your wedding maybe you should be doing some stuff with Jared that would preclude hacking with me?"

The brief flash of levity was reassuring. Slightly. Maybe Lacey was just tired. Both she and Fitch had finished demanding university programs in the spring and gone straight into labour-intensive summer jobs. They were preparing for a fifteen-hour drive. Maybe she sounded tired, because she was.

Still, it's important to Meg to be there when Lacey arrives. Being at the dock to wave her home might be a purely symbolic move ... but as Meg knows from the leaf pendant Jared gave her, that she's worn around her neck for so long, symbols can be powerful.

Lacey

GRANITE OUTCROPPINGS. And brick houses. Concession roads laid out in grid formation.

Things she would never have told anyone she'd miss about home, but now, as she sees them again, there's a click of familiarity, like a puzzle piece slotting into its proper spot, so cleanly there's no possible doubt it belongs where it is.

There are also the things she always knew she'd miss. The island as a whole, their farm in particular and, even more specifically, the little barn which she always remembers as snug and warm, with Salem waiting for her in it.

Of course she misses Salem – although she knows Meg's taking good care of the mare while Lacey's away.

And she misses Meg, and Jared, and her dad, and her brother who is, actually, much less annoying since he and Bridget moved in together (Will and Bridget, as responsible home-owners – Lacey can hardly believe it).

She doesn't ever say these things out loud to other people, though, because the obvious answer would be "move back," but … Fitch.

She looks at his profile as he holds their old station wagon straight in its lane on the highway. She watches his long, strong fingers flex and relax on the steering wheel. She notes the length of his hair, which she quite likes – curling around his ears and neck and onto his forehead.

Lacey knows there are places deep in Fitch's heart that he misses too. She knows the hilly terrain he grew up in, and the small, cold lakes that dot it, and the tiny-and-adorable, tourist-trapping villages are things he's putting off seeing so he can come to this wedding which is so important to her. She also knows that's part of why they went to school so far away. It seemed logical back when they made the decision – that it was only fair for them to each give up something they love to live somewhere new, fresh, neutral.

When they each had the chance to study exactly what they wanted in Nova Scotia it seemed ideal. They'd go far away, but they'd do it together. Surely, by the time they graduated they'd have the perspective they needed to fig-ure out where and how to move forward together.

Because that's clear – they're going to go forward to-gether. Someone could give Lacey all the things she's been missing on a platter and if Fitch wasn't part of the deal, she'd never be happy.

The great news is she doesn't have to miss anything. Not right now, and not for the next few days, because they're rolling onto the ferry. The car gives the familiar *thunk-thunk* as they transition from the ramp to the boat deck. The ferry worker – a distant cousin on Lacey's dad's side – holds up her palm to show they're close enough to the bumper of the car in front, and Lacey feels tension she didn't know she was holding drain out of her body.

Slate

BREATHE.

It's all she's been focusing on. Trying to breathe.

The first thing she does is go to yoga.

She underperforms there, though. She can't get her diaphragm to do what it's supposed to. Her breathing is stubbornly shallow and quick and, of course, the scariest and most militant yoga instructor is leading the class.

The yogi walks through the mats and, when she reaches Slate's, murmurs, "Breath is foundation. Breath is life. Breath is all."

The stress of not even getting the fundamental act of breathing right, along with the pressure of being watched, amps Slate's anxiety up and makes her gasp for air.

Afterward, she goes to her parents' house and that's an even bigger mistake. In her head she thinks, *I'll go and tell them I lost my job and they'll say, "That's OK, Slatey," and "We're always here for you," and "You'll end up getting a much better job."* She's supposed to be smart, so she's not sure why she hasn't figured out that her IRL parents are not the same as the dream parents who live in her mind.

What actually happens is her mom launches straight into her current favourite passive-aggressive topic – Meg's wedding. "I told Sally Henderson that you're wearing one of your own dresses to be Meg's bridesmaid and she thought that was very odd, but I just told her, 'Meg's a dear, but she's never thought much about fashion,'" followed by, "Did you remember to give Meg the name of Sally's niece who's a wedding photographer? I'd hate for Meg to regret not choosing a real professional," then, "Of course, we always thought we'd be invited to Meg's wedding, but I suppose she can only afford so many guests."

Slate's reliving her supervisor calling her into the supply closet because nobody at the clinic has an office with walls and a door. She'll never forget the look on the woman's face as she said, "I'm afraid it's bad news ..."

"Slate?"

"Huh? Sorry, what mom?"

"Where is Meg going on her honeymoon?"

"What? I don't know if they're taking one, Mom."

"Well, aren't you the maid of honour?"

"Not exactly. I don't think Meg's having a maid of honour."

"How can you not know? The wedding's this weekend."

"I think we're all just equal bridesmaids."

"That's ridiculous. There has to be a maid of honour. Have you and Meg had an argument?"

"Of course not. It's just not that important."

"What could more important than a girl's wedding?" her mother asks.

"Oh, I don't know, Mom. Maybe her actual marriage? Maybe their life together trying to keep a family farm alive?"

"Hmpf!" As soon as her dad puts down his paper and makes that noise, Slate realizes her mistake.

"Heavily subsidized by the taxpayers. Farmers. Always complaining, even though the government is shoring them up at the same time as they're making it impossible for businesses to thrive, taking away their profitability by jacking up the minimum wage."

Slate walked right into this topic – one of her dad's favourite lectures – but his rant has come in time to remind Slate of what will be in store as soon as she tells her parents about her job being cut.

Far from the unconditional sympathy she came here seeking, there would be statements about how the country's going downhill, fast. Driven by the government she voted for. So, really it's her own fault she lost her job.

Just as well she figured that out on her own without having to hear it from them.

Because that would only tighten her chest, make the oxygen harder to come by, and make it near-impossible to get through the whole story of funding cuts, lost grants, and the legal aid clinic having to lay off half their staff.

Lay her off from the job she's adored every single day since she started.

So, she doesn't explain. She just lies and says the oppressive humidity has given her a migraine. As she leaves she thinks she'll probably actually have a migraine if this shortness of breath persists.

At home she reads her bills and wonders how she's going to pay them, and that's when she first notices the physical sensation of the weight on her chest. The cat twines in and out of her legs, and when she thinks about her responsibility to feed him, the pressure doubles.

She falls asleep, but wakes up in the middle of the night, gasping for air.

In the morning, when she sees stars while eating her breakfast cereal, she decides she has to do something.

She remembers her mom asking if she and Meg have had an argument. It's true they haven't, but Slate also hasn't spent nearly as much time with Meg as she'd like to lately. Yes, Meg's wedding is low-key, and yes, considering Slate's workload at the clinic, Meg was completely fine with her arriving the day of, but now that there's no Slate-at-the-clinic, no workload, there's also no reason Slate can't head to the island a day early.

Driving, she's quite sure, is not a good idea in her current state, so she goes online, buys an economy train ticket, and uses the time before departure to clean her apartment, pack her bags – including her long-time favourite dress which will be her bridesmaid's dress – and ask her neighbour to take care of the cat.

"Doing something fun?" the woman asks.

"Going to my best friend's wedding."

"Oh! That is fun! Don't rush back. I'm happy to feed the cat as long as you like and I can bring her into my apartment if she seems lonely."

"Thank you," Slate says. She may not get unconditional support from her mother, but at least somebody gives it to her.

The train is OK because everyone has to wear masks so she can tell herself it's her mask keeping her from getting a deep breath in.

Plus, she loves the sideways-sliding scenery, the *shush-shush-click-click* of the rails, and the autumn sun slanting in, seemingly carrying with it hues of all the orange, and red, and yellow maples it's touched along the way.

In the taxi in Kingston, again with the mask, she tells herself the shallow breaths are still fine –– still normal.

The ferry's in as the taxi drops her off, ramp down, cars crawling on.

She walks along the gangway onto the boat, finds a spot on the rails, pulls her mask off, leans as far as she can out over Lake Ontario and, for the first time since she carried her spider plant out of her tiny cubicle, breathes all the way in – to the bottom of her lungs – then all the way out again.

Austen

ONE OF THE OSPREYS that lives on the nesting plat-form by the ferry dock soars over Austen's head and she wants the vision of it to lift her heart.

This time last year it would have. This time last year, so many things could shoot her full of happiness. The red hull of a laker pushing through the morning mist on the St. Lawrence. Soba noodles in a bowl with tahini sauce. The morning moon hanging low over the fields.

Rand.

The smell of his hair as they share a pillow. The slow, crooked smile that takes over his face when he sees her. His hands, working wood, sweeping a broom, holding power tools.

Her inner delight in Rand is there, deep down. She knows it's just being held under by a heap of scar tissue, but there's no way Rand can know that. Emotions, and spontaneity, and joy have been hard for her to feel, or show this last while.

That's why she's here right now. To pick up a parcel off the boat. One that contains Rand's new drill. More powerful, with a longer-lasting battery. She listened to Rand talk about it, and she said she'd come get it because these are the paltry things she can do to let him know she still loves him, even if she's no fun to live with day-to-day.

So, she waits at the dock – standing in the only patch of shade she could find which, to be honest, doesn't really help when the air itself feels like a sauna – and watches the ferry glide in. She lets herself think of what it would be like if her sister was here.

This is one of the things her therapist suggested – "You don't have to let go of her if you don't want to," – and it was a huge relief.

It's not something she can talk about with her mom because her mom is all about accepting Eliot's death, and building a legacy from it, and having good come out of it.

But that's another thing the therapist said – "Everyone grieves differently, and everyone is allowed to."

If she wants to picture her sister standing next to her, with her hair curling wildly around her face like it always did in the humidity of the summer, saying, "Who died and made you Rand's slave?" she's permitted to do just that. And if she wants to imagine answering, "Rand and I are a team. He's been spending all his spare time in the paddock at Kurt's fixing up the shelter so I can keep Mac at home if I want," then that's perfectly fine too.

"Aah, so you love him," Eliot would say, and before Austen could answer she'd add something like, "Fair enough," and it would have meant *I love you* and *I want you to be happy.*

Playing with her sister's memory this way is one of the things that gives Austen a smidgen of happiness and as long as it does, she plans to keep doing it.

Which is a relief, because she experiences Eliot everywhere. She feels her in the osprey winging in from the river – she believes her sister is free like that now. She sees her in the child being handed an ice cream cone from the ferry line food truck – Eliot loved ice cream and now that she can never get fat, in Austen's mind, her sister can eat all the ice cream she wants.

Austen sees Eliot in the girl standing against the railing of the boat shading her eyes to look up at a tall, lean guy with a tousle of blond hair falling across his forehead. It's not that the girl looks like Eliot, but the way the guy's laughing at something she's said. Eliot was so, so funny. More than one guy fell for her because of her wicked wit.

Her mother always used to say, "The way to a man's heart is through his brain – that's how your father and I got together."

Eliot would always answer, "Well, the way you cook, it definitely wasn't going to be through his stomach."

Watching Eliot make an entire group of people laugh at school, then seeing a guy from that group start showing up at their house after school made Austen think the way to a guy's heart – or anyone's for that matter – was more likely through their sense of humour. The fact that none of those relationships ever went anywhere also made Austen wonder if maybe Eliot had no interest in attracting guys, full stop.

She never asked, though. It didn't seem important. There would be time for that later. Now, though – now that she can never ask ... well ... she shakes her head and watches the girl throw her head all the way back and laugh at the blond guy, and thinks *good for her.*

Now Austen has to stop her daydreaming because the ferry hand's made the boat fast to the dock, looping the impossibly thick ropes around the mooring bollard, and there are only a few minutes while the loads switch over when she can retrieve Rand's prize drill.

There's usually a stack of parcels to the left of the ramp. Today's no exception, but she can't see one with the distinct orange tape of the building supplier where Rand shops so often, nor anything addressed to Rand.

"Austen!"

She turns to face a rosy-cheeked guy wearing a high-visibility vest, holding out the orange-taped box she's been looking for.

"This came on last-minute and I got busy and forgot to stick it up here." He looks at the label, "At least, I assume it's what you're here for – picking up another toy for Rand."

"Thanks Hank." She takes the heavy box from him, and turns away.

"Wait," he says. "There's this, too. It was with the FedEx deliveries."

He holds out a large padded envelope. It hardly weighs anything. Austen furrows her brow and checks the return address. **Past Times Vintage**. Her heart twinges.

It was Eliot's thing. She always liked to be ready for a run, and spent most of her days in stretch fabrics of some sort, but when she did have an event to dress for, it had to be vintage.

It was weeks ago now – no, more like a couple of months – that Austen had been clearing her inbox and found a message from her sister with a link and a one-liner: **My birthday's coming. Just sayin'** .... The link went to a vintage seller on Etsy and was for a pretty white dress. Unlike most of Eliot's dream dresses, it was affordable, and on a whim, Austen had clicked the "Pay direct by Pay-Pal" link.

And forgotten about it.

And now, here it is. And Meg's wedding is tomorrow. And they're supposed to wear whatever they want.

It's as Austen's wondering if it will even fit, and how it would look on her, that an ancient station wagon rolls toward them and Hank salutes the young woman in the passenger seat, whose face comes alive with a broad smile. She leans forward and cranks the window down. "Oh! Hankers! Great to see you!"

"Hey Lace, your dad told me you were coming home! It hasn't been the same without you."

They exchange farewell waves as the car clanks off the ferry.

"Lacey Strickland?" Austen asks.

He nods. "Jared's cousin. Have you never met her?"

"Not yet, but I guess I will soon enough. Anyway, thanks for the package."

She texts Rand as she heads back to the car. **Got your drill.**

The answer vibrates back once she's sitting in the driver's seat. **Love you!**

She stares at the words. Blinks hard. She knows she loves Rand.

There's no reason not to love Rand. Every day his talent becomes more apparent. He makes more beautiful things and he enjoys his work more.

He keeps working hard to stay away from alcohol. Even though Austen's pretty sure with him it was less about the actual drinking, and more about his own sense of self worth, still, he doesn't take any chances.

He's just as gorgeous as ever. Probably moreso. His stunning grey-green eyes stand out even more than they used to in his work-lean face.

Austen pictures him now, at the job he's been working on out at the foot of the island. Assembling a traditional Eastern Ontario cedar split fence in the old authentic way. No nails, with the rails looking random and natural, but carefully placed to be as solid as anything. His skilled hands working the wood, the sun catching his hair.

And his kindness. Since Eliot died, he's been there for her, for her family. She and Rand have had Shaw to stay several weekends to give him a change of scenery from the house in the city and to give her parents some time and space to work through their grief.

He gives her space, too. Sure, she does her best – tries to do her part – running the business end of things for Rand. Maintaining his client lists, sending out quotes, invoicing for jobs, and balancing the books. She's just about managed to keep up with all that, but the rest of it – the main reason she moved here with Rand – her proposal that she refinish and paint old furniture; that she add another dimension to the business, well that's all come to nothing so far.

Rand's never said anything. Rand's given her room and time, but she feels the pressure for herself. At some point she needs to earn money. At some point she needs a purpose.

In her peripheral vision, Austen notices the white van with the hotel logo on the side pulling out of the parking area. She's been picking up casual shifts at the hotel pub and yesterday they offered her full-time hours if she wants them.

Does she want them?

Not really.

Does she want to refinish the wooden bed Rand brought home from his last job? "It was in the barn," he said. "They said I could take it. I thought you might want to stop sleeping on a futon." She *wants* to want to, but when it comes right down to it, she can't pick a colour, or even start sanding it – she can't picture the finished product, and without that vision she can't start.

Does she love Rand? She reads his words again, and she believes them – he loves her – and she's sure she loves him too, but she just can't express it.

It's not just him – it's everyone. Like she's lost the ability to experience emotion.

The only thing she knows for sure, she wants for sure, she can feel for sure, is that she wants Eliot back.

And that's not going to happen.

Austen sighs and selects a smiley face to send back to Rand, and that's when a knock on her car window scares her half to death.

At least her heart feels something, if only that it might jump out of her chest.

Meg

IT'S BECAUSE of the new ferry that Meg was able to ride Hops to the dock.

Bigger, sleeker, and electric, it's being built halfway around the world. While it's under construction, the docks both here and on the mainland need to be retrofitted, and that's why the old ferry is using the winter dock for the duration.

A lot of people complain. The winter dock is down a dead-end spur off the highway, nestled between two farms. If you're waiting in line you can't go to the post office, or the general store like you can from the main ferry dock.

But, sure enough, somebody's opened a food truck by the side of the road, and there are temporary bathrooms, and Meg can get here across the fields on horseback, to stand on a ridge and watch the boat unload.

The boat is close enough to make out the bow wave, but not enough to read the letters above it, which Meg knows spell out **Wolfe Islander III**. Meg jumps off Hop's back, unbuckles one side of his bit and lets him lower his head and graze while she waits for the ferry to dock.

She scratches his withers, then runs her hand along his neck under his mane. He really is amazingly fit. "Hot" doesn't even begin to describe today – made worse by the thick humidity that almost never makes the jump from the mainland. Meg knows her hair is wet under her helmet. Her shirt dark under her protective vest. Yet this horse's neck isn't much more than damp, despite all his running.

At least here, next to the river, there's a weak breeze. She turns him into it while fanning the hem of her t-shirt.

Her phone buzzes and she checks the screen. **Mom.**

Oh no.

She doesn't want to answer the phone because her mom will make her feel bad.

She feels bad because she doesn't want to answer her mom's call.

As usual she has to decide which kind of bad she's prepared to feel.

The boat's navigating between the mooring dolphins. Answering the phone now would add the extra guilt of rushing the conversation, so she lets the call ring out.

She's not at all surprised when a text buzzes in just a minute later. **Meg, I just got off the phone with the restaurant. They can extend our reservation tonight to four if you and Jared would like to join us. Or, they had a last-minute cancellation for their private room so you could bring the wedding party and have a proper rehearsal dinner after all. Your father and I would pay, of course.**

No.

Meg's lost count of how many times, and how many ways she's said it.

No thank you.

I don't think so.

It's nice of you to offer.

Jared and I have talked about it and we don't want a rehearsal dinner.

No. No. No. No.

Meg sighs. **Remember we're having the bonfire tonight instead of a rehearsal dinner? It's all set. Like I said before, you and Dad are welcome to come.**

The text comes back. **We'll see what time it is when we're finished dinner.**

Which means no. Which is fine with Meg. Just as she and Jared wouldn't be comfortable in a low-lit restaurant with candles on the tables, her mother would never be happy with campfire blowing into her clothes and hair, and roasted marshmallows sticking her fingers together.

Before Meg can reply there's another text. **Betsy told me you're planning on using paper napkins? I contacted a linen rental service in Kingston and they can supply cloth napkins which your father and I can pick up when we go over for dinner.**

Meg sighs. She's pretty sure the cloth napkins her mom's picking up won't look right with the butcher paper they're using as table runners, but she also doesn't care deeply about the napkin situation. If she lets her mom do this, it might keep her from mentioning, yet again, that Meg should really be staying at Betsy and Carl's B&B along with her parents tonight – "It's very odd for you and Jared to just stay at home together as though nothing special is happening tomorrow." It might also prevent her from asking more about Meg's dress.

"Oh, god, yes," she tells Hops. "I have to message Slate about that!"

Hops turns one ear toward her but keeps tearing at the lush grass.

She sends a quick reply to her mother. **If picking up the napkins isn't too much trouble, then please go ahead.** Her finger hovers over "send" and she sighs at the insincerity of it even as she adds. **Thanks!**

Then she messages Slate. **Small near-disaster which I know you can avert for me. The place I ordered my dress from sent me an email a couple of weeks ago. I assumed it was a shipping notification and didn't open it. This morning, I realized the dress hadn't arrived and opened the message to see it was a cancellation of my order … I know, I know … can you bring a couple of extra dresses for me to try on? I really love that light blue one you wore for your graduation party. You're the best!**

"There!" Meg tells Hops. "Problem dealt with. I like Slate's dress way more than the one I ordered anyway, so that's perfect, and here we go, the ferry's unloading!"

Shielding her eyes from the sun, the first thing Meg notices is Hank's face. It lights up in a delighted smile, and she follows his gaze to the window of a beaten-up station wagon. The kind with wood paneling on it. Lacey and Fitch's.

It's no surprise at all that Hank's face looks like Christmas morning. Catching a glimpse of Lacey can do that to you. She's so pretty and sunny. You'd have to work hard not to love her.

Meg feels the surge right now – the happiness she first felt way back, early on, when she'd already fallen for Jared but they weren't an item. She remembers meeting Lacey, and how Lacey thought she, Meg, was the best thing ever, and how she never tried to hide it.

There were hard moments that summer – Meg was sometimes full of uncertainty – but Lacey's frank affection could always anchor her.

The car's rolling forward now. Meg can see Fitch's handsome profile in the driver's seat.

From her elevated spot on the grassy rise, she jumps up and down and waves.

She didn't text ahead of time because, as much as she'd planned to be here, and wanted to be here, working with horses – especially young ones – makes so many things unpredictable. The fox, for example. That could have derailed the entire ride.

At the last second she wonders if she should try to ping Lacey – if Lacey will even get the message **Look up on the ridge!** – but just as she's wondering, and thinking how silly she'll feel if she rode all the way over here and Lacey never knows, the car slows. Fitch points. The horn toots twice, then a long, lean, tanned arm appears from the passenger side window, waving and waving.

That's it – that's all Meg wanted.

This simple trip has already ticked a few things off Meg's list.

Hops has been exercised, and he's faced a fear and moved past it.

She's had a mental break from wedding details, because even a wedding as simple as the one she and Jared are planning has its moments – especially now that her mom's on the island.

Lacey's been properly greeted. Most importantly, Lacey's back home – even if just for a short while – which reminds Meg … *home* … *Lacey* … Jared has a bonfire planned for tonight and she'd better get back to help him set it up.

She swings back into the saddle and is pleased to find, despite the sweltering temperatures and the long run he's already had, Hops is keen to jump back up to a canter.

This horse is going to be a good one.

Slate

THERE ARE MANY magical things about this ferry, this harbour, and the windswept island and charming city they connect.

One of them is undoubtedly the seemingly never-ending parade of sailboats which are part of CORK – Canadian Olympic Regatta Kingston. Slate can't tell any of the boats from each other, and she has no idea if she's watching youth races or Olympic-class competition, but she does know it's all captivating – the spray of sails across the water. Slate thinks a fleet of sailboats is nearly as pretty as a herd of horses.

A woman lifts a little girl to the rail next to Slate. The child points. "I like those sails, Mommy!"

Slate looks more closely and notices all the sails are made of large transparent expanses trimmed with broad orange or red borders. "They are pretty, aren't they?" she says to the little girl.

"Do you know what kind of boat they are?" the girl asks.

"I don't," Slate says. She doesn't like not knowing. She'll Google it later. She's watching the girl run off and the mother hurry after her when she hears a voice from behind her.

"They're twenty-niners."

She turns around and is grinning before she can think about it.

Everything about the guy standing in front of her makes her happy. His eyes sparkle. His teeth are ridiculously white – and even – and she can see all of them because of his wide smile. He has really beautiful eyebrows and an expanse of smooth forehead leading to a tumble of blond hair. It's half wavy and half messy.

"Were you by any chance just sailing one of those?"

"I wish! They're great boats – incredibly fast." He runs a hand through his hair. "It's the hairstyle that made you ask, right? My sister's always telling me I look like I fell in." He gives a little half-bow. "I didn't know I'd meet anyone I'd want to impress today."

"You already have," Slate says. "Just by telling me what kind of boat those are. It bugs me not to know stuff like that."

He laughs. "Well, I can't promise much else, but I can tell you lots about sailboats."

"OK," she says. "Those little ones over there – what kind are they?"

It's the engines cutting that brings Slate back to reality. The trip passed in a wink with the sailing expert guy pointing out 49ers, and Lasers, and Optimists. She's already half in love with the idea of sailing an "Opti" as he calls them. They look as jaunty as their name and he assures her they're as solid as a bathtub.

The sudden quiet stops them both mid-laugh. "Oh, gosh," Slate says. "I guess that's your cue."

He does that hand-running-through-hair thing again that, each time, produces a new and more interesting hairstyle. "Excuse me?"

She points to the keys hanging from his pocket. "You have a car on the boat? You need to drive it off?"

"Yes! Absolutely. I do have a car. You?"

She shakes her head. "Nope. I walked."

"OK, well it was nice to meet you."

"Likewise. Sailing an Opti is going on my bucket list."

People are streaming down from the upper deck, jockeying for position so they can be first off the boat. Slate stays where she is and the guy gets jostled away, toward the lanes of cars. He lifts his hand – holding the keys – and she lifts hers in response.

That was nice.

It was ten minutes that felt like an hour ... but in a good way. For that space of time, Slate forgot completely about lost jobs, and oblivious parents. About her best friend's looming wedding, which will be fun, but is still a responsibility.

Also, about the fact that she doesn't have a ride to Meg's.

Shit.

Given the shock Slate's system has taken in the last twenty-four hours, and given that she made it this far via taxi, and train, and another taxi, she's been feeling pretty proud of herself.

It's not that she didn't know there was no taxi service on the island, it's that she expected to disembark in the compact little village where she had a vague idea she could go to the general store and somebody would give her the number of some island resident who did down-low taxi driving.

But now, in her post-sailboat-discussion daydreamy state, she's let the masses pour off ahead of her, and has walked into a rapidly emptying parking lot paved between two farm fields. As cars roll past her, she automatically starts walking. Even though she doesn't know where they've docked, or where she's heading, standing still doesn't seem like an option.

That's when she spies the pretty girl sitting in one of the last parked cars. She looks friendly and normal, and Slate heard the ferry worker saying Jared's name to her. At the time, Slate took it as a sign that everyone knows Meg and Jared, and she'd have no problem snagging a lift.

Now she takes it as her last chance.

Slate looks over her shoulder to make sure she's not stepping out in front of a car as she turns toward her potential saviour. Her hand flies to her chest because she *is* stepping out in front of a car. A Jeep, to be precise. One that's seen better days.

Happy-smiling-sailor-guy is behind the wheel and her spirits automatically lift again at the sight of him.

"Hey," he says. "When you said you were walking, I didn't think you meant literally walking to your final destination. You do know the closest house is at least a kilometre away, right?" He points at the wheelie suitcase she's holding. She wonders if he's noticed the bead of sweat that just rolled down her temple.

"Um, yeah. I feel kind of silly. Every time I've taken the ferry we've docked in the village."

He nods. "You're not the only one to get caught – there's at least one person on most trips. The boat's docking here while the docks in the village are under construction. Is that where you need to go? The village? I can give you a lift, no problem."

"Well, actually, I'm heading to my friend's place. It's just that I thought I'd be more likely to be able to get a lift from the village."

"OK. The island's not that big. I'll take you to your friend's place instead. Where is it?"

"Honestly, I don't know the address – are there even addresses over here? Her name's Meg Traherne. She lives with Jared Strickland. Do you know them?"

Slate's sure he does, because his open, merry expression freezes and his tanned skin pales. She has no idea what that's about, and maybe it's best not to find out. She glances sideways to make sure the girl's still parked there. "I don't want to inconvenience you. I think I can probably get a lift ..." She steps sideways and knocks on the girl's window.

"Don't be silly. It's no problem at all. I know where the farm is – does that work?"

Slate hesitates. "It's just ... for a second there you looked ... I don't know. Not good."

"The thing is ..." He lets go of the steering wheel, rubs his eyes, and when he looks at her again, the frank friendliness is back. "I'm home for my grandfather's funeral so, I have these moments."

Moments. Slate can understand those. "I'm sorry."

"Thank you."

She turns back and makes eye contact with the girl in the car. *Sorry*, she mouths, then opens Adam's passenger door and points inside before finishing with a thumbs up. As she buckles herself into the seat, she says, "Maybe on the way you can tell me about your grandfather?"

***

They pull up at the end of the farm driveway much too soon. Slate was able to shed her troubles yet again, while he was telling her about his larger-than-life grandfather. About how everyone on the island knew him. About how he pretty much had to learn to sail because his grandfather ran the ferry to the smaller island where he grew up and, as a teenager, if he ever wanted to get around without his grandfather knowing about it, the only way was to sail himself.

Something tugs at Slate's mind a couple of times. Something familiar about the story. She's happy to ignore the feeling, though. It's nice to be with this undemanding person and his funny stories.

With the Jeep stopped next to the mailbox that says **Strickland**, Slate feels the same way she used to when she and Meg went to country fairs as teenagers, and their turn on the bumper cars would come to an end.

One minute it was all laughter, and chaos, and happy distraction, then the next everything went quiet and you had to climb out of your car to walk on slightly unsteady legs to the exit.

"So," she says.

"Well," he says.

"Thank you. It was really nice of you to drive me here. And I'm very sorry to hear about your grandfather. I'm sure the funeral will be lovely."

"I think it will be. Meg and Jared's wedding is tomorrow in the hall, then my grandfather's reception is there the next day."

"Oh, so you do know Meg and Jared fairly well." Slate's wondering if he's invited to the wedding. Her mind is whirling ahead to the dress she brought, and how she might make a little extra effort with her hair, and how amazing he'd look in dressy clothes, and how much fun it would be to dance with him.

He nods. Clears his throat. Holds out his hand. "I'm Adam."

She takes it and answers automatically. "Slate."

Then freezes. Holds his hand. Stares into his eyes. "Oh."

Sailing. A ferry to another, smaller island. *Adam.* "Oh," she repeats.

"Oh, yes," he says.

***

Adam's driving away, and Slate's head is spinning as she walks up the gravel driveway with the wheeled suitcase bumping and rattling behind her.

Shit.

Shit, shit, shit, shit, shit.

When was the last time she slept with a guy? DA:TD (don't answer: too depressing).

And, sure that's partly because of the all-encompassing nature of her (former) work, but more significantly because of just not meeting anyone who interested her.

Adam has definitely interested her. And now she doesn't even have a job to get in the way. She could stay on this island for weeks and weeks, letting Adam teach her how to sail an Opti and teaching him a thing or two …

A pang of desire shoots through her and she closes her eyes against it, and squeezes her temples, because all that would be possible if her best friend hadn't dated Adam, and her husband-to-be hadn't punched him. She shakes her head. "Of all the crossings of all the ferries in all the province … aarrgghh!"

"Slatey! Slate-my-girl! Super-duper Slate! You came to the wrong place, too!"

Slate lifts her eyes and blinks to focus on the also-very-attractive guy running toward her who she also won't be touching with a ten-foot pole – also, as it happens, because of Meg, but this time because he's her brother.

"Cam!" She drops the handle of her bag and flings her arms wide to be swept up in his long, strong arms. She lets him swing her off her feet before placing her down again.

Not that the frustration about Adam's gone, but she's genuinely pleased to see Cam. Cam's like that. A lifter-of-spirits. A force for good. Overly energized. Maddening to some, but welcome to her, especially right now.

"What's this about being in the wrong place?" There are paddocks full of horses all along the driveway and in the closest one is Salem's very distinctive appaloosa backside.

"The house?" Cam prompts. "The converted schoolhouse? Five-hundred square feet that makes my sister happy and drives my mother crazy because it's not a four-bedroom centre hall on the next street over from my parents' house?"

Slate nods. "I've seen all the construction photos, of course, but ... it isn't here?"

Cam laughs. "You have a better excuse than me. You thought you were coming to the right place. I knew better but ..." He mimes some sort of explosion going off beside his head. "Goat brain."

"Goat brain?"

"Our dairy goats are kidding. It's madness back on the farm. Haven't had a full night's sleep for a week."

"You have dairy goats?"

"Among other things. Come on – let's put your silly little city bag in the truck and I'll drive you over to Meg's actual house."

Meg

MEG OFTEN THINKS the outdoor shower is her favourite thing about the converted schoolhouse she shares with Jared.

Then she sits on the couch in front of the French doors that look out over the river, or she wipes down the corrugated metal kitchen backsplash – made with material left over from the loafing shed she and Jared built onto the side of the barn in the spring, or she lies in bed with the windows open at either end of the upstairs loft and feels the breeze moving through their bedroom, and she loves all those things, too.

The outdoor shower, though, on days like today, is special. Everything's sun-warmed – the water, the shampoo, and Meg's shoulders as she rinses until the water runs clear down her body, over her feet, and into the river rocks beneath the raised wooden shower floor.

Its vantage point gives her a view over the river which offers a very quick glimpse of the ferry, about halfway through its crossing.

It also means, when she hears tires crunching on the primitive drive of two worn tire ruts with grass growing between them, she can turn to see who's arriving. She expects Jared, but instead of his familiar truck, it's a blue one she knows almost as well.

"Cam!" When you have an outdoor shower, you also always have to have a bathrobe handy, and she shrugs into hers now, letting her hair drip down the back.

"Oh! And Slate! How did you find each other? What are you doing here?" She hugs them both and they hug her back, and this is what her mom doesn't understand; that the reason she's not worried about the wedding itself – the actual moment – is because it's all this good stuff around it that she wants. Her favourite people all together on the island for one weekend. Slate arriving with Cam is the perfect illustration of that.

"I found her at the farm," Cam's saying.

"Something happened in the city so I left early," Slate's saying.

"Bring your things in! I'll get you drinks! I'll put on clothes!" Meg's saying.

A couple of minutes later they're all staring at the sleeping cubby under the stairs. It's spacious for one person, cozy for a couple … awkward for two people who aren't supposed to be sleeping together. "I'm sorry," Slate says. "I didn't think at all. I'm sure there's a B&B or a hotel …"

"Don't be silly," Meg says. "There's room for everyone."

Cam shakes his head. "There really isn't, Sis. As much as I'm a one-Lynsey man these days, in quarters that tight, with someone as cute as Slate, I can't be responsible for the moves my unconscious self might put on your best friend."

Meg wrinkles her nose. "Um, yuck … I also wouldn't want to be responsible for that. We can easily put a camping mattress on the floor in our room upstairs."

"Oh yeah, that's a great idea."

"You say that like you mean the exact opposite."

"Oh, Meg, not even for you – my favourite sister –"

"Only sister," Meg points out.

"Favourite sibling."

"Still only."

"Not even for you can I listen to any more of Mom's despair that you're spending the night sleeping with the man you're going to spend every night for the rest of your life sleeping with. Do you know I had to talk her out of booking you a hotel room and 'surprising' you by sending a limo to pick you up at the barn and take you there, whether you liked it or not?"

Slate who's known Meg and Jared's mom nearly as long as they have, lifts an eyebrow. "How did you manage that?"

"I told her there was a word for that, and it was kidnapping." He turns to Meg. "But honestly, if she finds out that not only did you sleep at home, in your own bed, with your fiancé, but that I was bunking on your floor, she'll kidnap both of us."

"I wasn't thinking of you," Meg says. "Your feet stink. I wanted Slate."

Slate shakes her head. "Nuh-uh. I'm also scared of your mom."

"I'll sleep in the barn," Cam says.

"You will not!" Slate says.

"Hey, what did I tell you about goat-kidding? Any sleep I've had in the last week has been in the barn. I find the aroma of hay very sleep-inducing."

"I can't take this cozy bed while you sleep in a barn," Slate insists.

Meg sighs. "I reckon he can. Besides, if he sleeps in the hayloft with the doors open, it'll be cooler than in the house." She pauses. "Although, of course, as Mom keeps telling me, there's lots of room at Betsy and Carl's. She and Dad are only using one of the guest rooms."

"No, no, no, and no." Cam's head-shaking is so vigorous, watching him gives Meg a headache. "I love all four of those people and I want to keep it that way by not sleeping under the same roof as them. I have a sleeping bag in the truck. I'll be fine."

Meg cranes past Cam to peer out the small round window over the guest bed. "Well, since that's settled you can help Jared barbecue our dinner. That's him pulling in now."

***

As Meg's stepping into clean shorts, Slate runs up the stairs to the loft. "Meg! I just read your text."

"What text?"

"This one." Slate holds up her phone: **Slate. Small near-disaster ...**

"Oh, yeah. I sent that while I was waiting for the ferry to come in so I could wave hello to Lacey."

"The ferry I was also on," Slate says.

"Oh. I see. I sent the text asking you to bring a dress when you were already on the ferry ... which means, no dress."

"I'm sorry, Meg."

"It's OK. I'm sure I have something I can wear."

"Are you?"

"Yes. I must. There's a whole end of the closet I never look at."

"Open it up, then."

Meg and Slate stand in the light-flooded loft with the closet doors wide open.

"You and I need to go dress shopping," Slate says.

"I mean ... I have a dress."

"That's – I'm guessing here – your all-purpose funeral dress." As Slate says "funeral," she thinks of Adam going to his grandfather's funeral. She wonders what he'll wear. Wonders if he'll try to tame his hair. Hopes not, then realizes of course it doesn't matter because she won't be there to see him.

"I wasn't suggesting I wear that dress. For one thing, it would be way too hot." Meg swipes her hand across her forehead. The refreshment of her shower has already worn off.

"Seriously, Meg, you need something to wear. We need to go over to Kingston tomorrow morning."

Meg sinks onto the bed. Drops her face into her hands. "I fully admit this is my fault. And I also admit I need a dress." She spreads her fingers and peeks through them. "But I still don't want to go shopping. The dress I thought I was getting was fine – there was nothing wrong with it. It's hard for me to find dresses with nothing wrong with them."

Slate drops down beside her. "Who knows – we might find something better. We'll go over first thing – as soon as the shops are open. We'll make a list of places to hit and we'll get back on the next boat. It'll be fine."

Meg sighs and leans against her friend. "Thanks, Slatey. Our rings are being cleaned, too. The jeweler was going to send them over on the boat tomorrow morning, but I guess we can pick them up while we're over."

Slate nods. "Yes. And take care of any other last-minute things like that. We'll have fun. I can get one of those amazing coffees from that cute coffee shop a block up from the dock."

Meg rolls her shoulders back, one at a time and smiles at Slate. "You're right. There's plenty of time. I was giving all the horses the day off anyway, with this heat ..."

"... and the fact that you're getting married."

Meg laughs. "That, too. It will make our wedding more memorable – that I chose my wedding dress on the actual day." She swivels to face Slate. "Now, you said something happened in the city. Tell me what it is ..."

Lacey

LOW-SLANTING SUN, a chorus of crickets, and the never-ending sigh of the island breeze.

The appaloosa mare, hind leg cocked, face pressed hard against her t-shirt.

Field, and trees, and water, and sky all within sight.

These things are how Lacey knows she's home. These and the deep feeling she has of not owing anyone anything. Of being good enough just as she is. Of belonging just because she's Lacey, and she's a Strickland, and she was born here, and she can always come back.

There's laughter in the distance. Men's laughter.

Jared's first, followed by Fitch's. It occurs to Lacey it's been a while since she's heard Fitch laugh like that. "See?" She straightens Salem's forelock. "Being here is good for him, too."

After a good, long visit with her chin resting on Salem's poll, the faintest whiff of campfire tickles Lacey's nostrils.

"Now I'm going to have to go," she tells the mare. "It's growing up with my brother that's done it. I live in fear of all the marshmallows being gone."

Salem's ears flick around and she shifts her weight, but not in a way that conveys any urgency – more like she's getting comfortable for a longer snuggle.

"I know, I know," Lacey says. "It's easy for you though. You're the boss mare. You're always going to get a share of the food."

She sighs, "Come on then," and takes a step. Salem rests her muzzle on Lacey's outstretched hand and ambles beside her as they pick their way across the paddock, through clumps of late-season wildflowers.

Hops, Salem's paddock-mate, watches their progress with forward-pitched ears and wide-flared nostrils, but there's no way he's going to join them. Salem's taught him his horsey role all too well. He's well below her in the pecking order so it would be crazy to leave the hay feeder while Salem's not there.

He's a handsome gelding, Lacey thinks, with the setting sun picking highlights out of his coat and making shadows that emphasize his lean muscles.

"I'd love to have a riding horse again," she tells Salem. The university's program horses that she takes care of are sweet and reliable, but they definitely don't thrill her.

And Night, the horse she brought home from camp when she first met Fitch has a home with a boy who taught him to rope calves and who has time to ride him every day.

It wasn't a particularly hard decision – "We'll always keep Salem," her dad said, "But we can't hold onto an endless stable of horses you're never going to ride."

Lacey knew that was fair, and she knew when, eventually, she did have time to ride and train a horse, she'd want to look for her dream horse – something brave and bold. She's always liked the idea of endurance riding, and she knows she'd need to find the right partner to be able to tackle that.

Still, maybe she'll ask Meg for a ride on Hops while she's home.

They get to the fence and Lacey reaches out to scratch Salem's withers. "This is where we part ways ... unless you want to come over to the fire."

The flames are visible now – dancing into the rapidly cooling and darkening air – and the campfire smell is strong.

Salem snorts.

"Yeah, that's what I thought." Lacey kisses the mare's forehead. "Night, pretty girl. I'll see you in the morning." She gives her one more kiss – "It's so nice to be able to say that!" – then scampers toward the fire. "OK, what did I miss? Are there marshmallows left? Please tell me there are marshmallows left!"

Fitch laughs and ushers her to an upturned log. Once she's sitting, he reaches behind her and puts a toasting fork into her left hand, with a marshmallow pushed onto each prong while he puts an entire bag of marshmallows into her right.

She blinks hard. Her eyes are stinging. This person. This perfect, perfect, person for her. She has to believe it will all work out; they'll figure out where to live and she'll figure out how to be happy no matter where she is, as long as Fitch – and Salem – are with her.

"It's the smoke." She says out loud, then crooks her finger to get Fitch to lean in more closely, and when he does, she whispers in his ear. "It's not actually the smoke."

"Is it me?" he asks.

She holds up her long fork and twists the toasty brown marshmallows on the end. "No ... it's the perfect marshmallow."

Fitch nods. "Mmm ... OK, I see."

She kisses his cheek. "I know you do."

Before Fitch can say anything else, an authoritative voice rises above the crackling of the logs, and the hum of conversation, and the chirping of the crickets. "Well, hello everybody! We were able to come after all."

Meg

OH NO. Meg feels terrible that those are the first words that enter her mind when her mother makes her grand entrance to the circle of light around the bonfire.

But she can't change it – they were. And at least she didn't say them out loud. Although a sideways glance tells her Slate knows what she was thinking.

This was supposed to be a low-key, casual, easy-going get-together. It was supposed to be fun.

Now her mother bustles in, asking, "Is there by any chance a lawn chair I can sit on? I don't want to get my pants dirty." When Jared asks if he can get her a drink from the cooler she asks, "Do you have a dry white wine?"

Jared pauses and Meg steps in. "No, Mom. We only have drinks that come in their own cans. There are a few kinds of beer and some soft drinks."

"Well, don't worry about that for now. Your father and I have each prepared a few words to say, so we might as well do that now and we can worry about drinks later."

Oh no. There it is again. This is the very definition of a lose-lose situation. She doesn't want her parents to hijack this low-key night into the formal rehearsal dinner they couldn't convince her to have in the restaurant in town, but she also doesn't want to have a confrontation with them on the night before her wedding.

"Wait just a minute! I'm afraid you haven't seen the agenda – it's not time for speeches, it's time for gifts."

Meg doesn't always love Cam's barging-in-where-angels-fear-to-tread personality, but at times like this, she adores it.

"Agenda?" Meg's mom's voice is flustered. "No, I didn't see it. And, gifts? I didn't know we were giving gifts tonight."

"Don't worry, Mom, there is no agenda and the gift-giving is just me, because my gift has been cooped up for long enough – it can't wait until tomorrow."

The words "cooped up" and "can't wait" give Meg a familiar flutter of Cam-induced anxiety. Cam lives his life based on good intentions and love. Like the first summer she lived here alone when she thought he was at a university biology research station and he appeared at the dock at their cottage sailing a boat she'd never seen before with a girlfriend she didn't know he had. Or, like when she got the call about his current living conditions. "I met a girl named Lynsey. We're looking after a farm in Lake Placid. It has chickens, and horses, and goats ..."

"Goat ..." Cam's saying now.

"Excuse me?" Meg says. She turns to Jared, and mouths, *Did I hear that right?*

He shrugs, and she turns back to her brother. "A goat?"

Cam holds out a small, bleating creature. It thrashes its legs, and makes eye contact with her, and she finds herself reaching out and gathering it in. Its belly is round and soft under her hand, and it pushes its hard head against her chest.

"It's a pygmy," Cam says. "You can name it."

"I'm just not sure what to say ..."

"You're welcome."

The goat has snuggled into Meg's arms and when Slate walks over and reaches out a hand, it tilts its head as though asking for a scratch. "Is this one of your dairy goats you were telling me about?" she asks Cam.

"Oh no. This one just showed up one day. Lyn said we're run off our feet as it is, so it couldn't stay. Then I thought of you!" He points to his sister.

"The thing is, Cam, I'm not completely sure we're equipped to take care of a goat."

He nods. "I hear you. That's the beauty of goats. They're self-sufficient. They'll find their own food if they have to. I'm pretty sure after a nuclear explosion you'd find goats and cockroaches running around."

"That's what's worrying me." Meg throws a glance at Jared who lifts his eyebrows and takes a sip of his beer. *He's your brother,* he mouths. Meg continues. "Won't just one goat be lonely?"

"Oh, there won't be just one for long – they're a bit like bunnies – the only explanation I can give is that they spontaneously reproduce."

"Fantastic," Meg says.

Slate leans in. "Would you rather have listened to your mother's speech?"

Meg hugs the warm little body tight to her. "I'll take the goat."

*****

It turns out well – it all turns out well. Austen seems to know how to handle Meg's mom. She sits next to her and listens while Meg's mom complains about how the restaurant canceled their dinner reservations. "... something about a tornado warning, so they wanted to close their patio ... asked to be moved inside but said all those tables were reserved ..."

Austen nods. "How frustrating."

"These tornado warnings never come to anything."

"Certainly inconvenient," Austen agrees.

With her problems vented, Meg's mom is free to move on to being charming, which she's very good at when she puts her mind to it. Meg watches as Jared settles in for a little chat with her. He's learned when to seize on his future mother-in-law's good moods and when to keep his distance.

A brush of fur and quick bleat tell her the goat's run by her again. He ... or she ... is doing circuits of the bonfire. So far, keeping a safe distance. She suspects he's been cleaning up all the marshmallows that get dropped in the dirt, or a little too overtoasted. Her suspicion is confirmed as she sees Rand lean forward to hold a marshmallow out for the small animal.

Rand's firelit face looks happy. She glances around at all of their faces – all their friends here, now, around them.

Lacey and Fitch – both roasting marshmallows just for Lacey to eat. Austen and Rand. With Austen boarding Mac here, Meg's seen how much the girl's been through lately, and how the big horse has helped her through it. And Rand, despite their rocky start, has become Jared's closest friend, and a huge asset to the farm – working as Jared and Rod's right-hand on anything that takes more than just the two of them.

Then Slate. It's been far too long since they've had time together. Meg's grateful she came straight here when life threw her a curveball.

She has a sudden urge to yell, "Let's just do it now!" This would be perfect. Telling Jared she loves him, and having him say it back, and saying, "We've said this in front of all of you, and we mean it, and that's what's important."

Except, of course, the hall is booked, and she does love the village hall with its whitewashed interior and long trestle tables, and the stage at the end. She loves how it's equipped for everything from school pageants, to community fundraisers, to weddings, to funerals, and how tomorrow it will be her wedding there.

And the food is all planned – much of it from local people, including, of course, a few of Betsy's famous pies.

And if she waits until tomorrow they'll have their rings – all clean and sparkling – and she'll have some kind of dress which, even if it isn't her favourite, will be one she chose with her best friend.

Although she's not sure who's going to look after the goat while they get married. Since Lynsey couldn't come, maybe Cam can bring it with him.

She supposes she can wait.

A lick of wind lifts her hair and leans the flames toward her.

It's the warmth of the fire that makes her realize the temperature's dropped. The sticky humidity has left the air.

Another huge gust rushes in, blowing the flames the other way this time.

Austen and Rand jump back, and Austen holds up her toasting fork. "My marshmallow has ash all over it!" Another one for the goat.

In the darkness one of the horses whinnies, then Squall – Rex's successor – hurtles into the circle of light cast by the fire and presses his body against Meg's legs.

Meg's trusted Squall's instincts ever since the night she met him, when he saved her from having a car accident in a blizzard, and tonight he's as on the ball as ever. Just a few seconds later, lightning splits the sky followed by a boom of thunder she can feel in her chest.

"Whoa ... were we expecting this?" Austen asks.

"Cold front chasing a warm front," Jared answers.

Sure enough, Meg runs her hands up and down her arms and finds the skin raised in goosebumps. The temperature must have dropped close to ten degrees from the swelter of the afternoon.

"We heard severe weather warnings on the radio all the way from Ottawa to here," Lacey says.

"Tornado warnings," Meg's mom adds.

The night is full of more smells than campfire now. Ozone and the cool, sharp scent of coming rain fill Meg's nostrils.

There's more than that, too. Tension. "I think we should put the fire out," she says.

"I don't think we'll have to," Rand points to where a fat raindrop has landed on the hot rocks around the fire and is sizzling to steam.

"The horses?" Lacey asks.

Meg nods. "The boarders come in overnight anyway, so they're already in the barn. The rest have access to the loafing barn, so let's go ahead and put some extra hay in there."

Lacey and Austen come to help her while the others pack up the vehicles and pour the bucket of water they always keep nearby on the fire.

Austen lugs a bale of hay from inside to the shed, while Lacey spreads a fresh layer of straw across the floor. Meg's only just refilled the hay feeder when Salem, Hops, Mac, and Meg's other project horses come crowding into the shelter.

"Look!" Lacey points to the small body balanced on Hops high back. "There's no way you're getting rid of that goat – he's settled in already."

The three of them smile until a rattle of rain across the metal roof snaps them back to reality.

"Let's roll this door closed so there's just enough space for them to get back out single file if they want to." Meg grabs the heavy door and turns to the other two. "Good?"

All three of them look at the dim, snug interior of the lean-to. "Good," Lacey and Austen say together.

Meg nods. "In that case, I think we'd better run for the cars. It's going to pitch down any minute."

Slate

MEG, JARED, SLATE and Squall are snug and dry in the house, sitting on the floor in front of the French doors looking out to the river, when the heavens open.

The whole yard's highlighted in a flash of lightning, and the thunder is so close it fills the space around them.

Squall noses under Jared's legs and the wind flings so much water against the doors that the world outside blurs.

Slate shivers. "I'm glad we're inside."

Meg shifts from one seat bone to the other, "I'm worried about the others."

"Text them," Jared suggests. "Ask them to ping you when they get home."

Slate thinks about the last guy she dated – back when she was just starting her job at the legal clinic. She was nervous then about everything. Was she making the right decision? Would she be good enough at her job? Should she check up on her vulnerable clients on the weekend to make sure they were OK?

"Get over it," he used to say. "Those people are lucky to have you." But he said it less as a compliment to her and more as an insult to them. "You need to forget about them on the weekend."

Slate soon liked her job much more than she liked him, and it's one of the things Slate loves about Jared; that he doesn't dismiss other people's worries.

Slate's even heard Meg's mom say it: "He's a good person."

Slate differs from Meg's mother in many ways, but Jared's kindness is one thing they can always agree on.

Slate watches Meg tap away at her phone, her face lit by intermittent lightning flashes.

She hears Squall give a low moan. She wonders how the new goat is doing.

She thinks of Adam. She's been thinking about him all night.

Would he validate her worries, or brush them off? She has no idea, but she'd love to have the chance to find out.

I mean, yes, she definitely likes the looks of him. She wants to know how his hands feel on her. How his lips feel on hers. But she also wants to hear more about his grandfather, and growing up on a smaller island off a larger island. She wants to know why he likes sailing so much.

It seems this is more than lust. And it happened all at once.

It's something she thought she was immune to. To be honest, it's the one part of Meg and Jared's relationship she's never been fully comfortable with. The whole "love-at-first-sight-from-the-seat-of-a-vintage-tractor" thing.

She's never told Meg this, of course. Meg would probably be surprised to hear her say it, since as teenagers it was always Slate encouraging Meg to have a little fun. Let herself have a crush. Kiss the guy.

Probably, ironically, to kiss Adam, once-upon-a-time.

Slate however, always had a firm line between crushes and anything more meaningful. Crushes could come and go. Real love had to grow.

Except, suddenly, in the trip of a ferry, she finds she's deeply interested in Adam in a way that feels much stronger than any crush she's ever experienced.

Meg holds up her phone. "Austen says there was a branch down on the driveway – Rand's soaking wet from dragging it out of the way. Lacey says she and Fitch drove through a patch of hail right on the far side of the village that put a few new dents in the old station wagon, but they're all home safe."

"In that case ..." Slate stretches, then rises. "I'm off to bed."

Meg follows her to the sleeping cubby and Slate looks up at her from her seat on the bed. "Am I a bad person for climbing into this ridiculously comfy bed while Cam's sleeping in a hayloft?"

"Cam's slept in way worse places. Besides, Cam gave me a goat for my wedding."

"It's really cute."

"People say the same thing about Cam."

"Your point being?"

"There's no going back from either of them. Once you've met Cam your life will never be the same and I suspect the same is true of that goat."

"Meaning, you're happy to leave your brother in the doghouse ... or the goat house ... while this storm rages on."

"Knowing Cam he's already asleep." Meg's face goes serious. "Are you OK? You've had a shock and we haven't really talked about it."

Slate waves her hand. "It's nice not to talk about it. It's nice to have other things to think about." Like Adam. For a fleeting second she considers coming clean to Meg. *I met a guy. I found him really intriguing. Then I found out he's Adam who you not-quite dated years ago. How would you feel if I call him?*

But no. Tomorrow is Meg's wedding. The next twenty-four hours is supposed to be about her. Slate will sleep on the whole Adam thing and maybe he'll lose his lustre overnight. Maybe she'll wake up and have no desire to see him again. And if she still wants to see him ... well she can ask Meg about it later. After all, it took her this long to meet him – this isn't exactly an urgent situation.

"I know. But it's still a shock to the system."

Slate blinks. Of course Meg had no idea she was daydreaming about Adam. She's still on their original topic of unemployment.

Slate sighs and lets Meg think it's entirely about the job. "You're right. It is a shock. And I have no idea what comes next."

"Take your time. Think it through. You have a lot of options."

Slate sighs. "I'm sure you're right, but I was just so happy there. Doing that work. Helping people."

"I know you were. And you're good at it. There'll be something else."

Slate looks at her. "I admire you, Meg. You're good at that – at seeing what comes along and going with it. I'm not. Never have been. I need a plan."

Meg snorts. "I know someone who thinks I'm the worst planner in the world – at least when it comes to my wedding."

Slate laughs. "But what would your mother do with her time if she couldn't worry about your life?"

The little round porthole window set into the wall above the bed lights up completely with a sheet of lightning.

"I thought it was easing off," Meg says. "But looks like it's turned back around on us."

Slate plumps her pillows. "That's fine with me. We're snug in here, the horses are snug in the barn – I'm sure Cam is too – and you know Lacey and Austen are safe, so we can just lie here and watch and listen. And tomorrow we'll get you a dress and you can get married!"

Meg's phone pings at the same time as a gust of wind wails around the house. They both tense. "What if ...?" Meg says.

"It's fine. It's nothing. Just check it ... Meg? What's wrong?"

"Oh. Sorry. It's not Lacey or Austen. It's ..." Meg holds the phone out for Slate to read the message.

Meg, just as I was coming up to bed, Betsy asked me which of your attendants is your maid of honour. I was embarrassed to tell her I didn't know. Please tell me you have chosen one and she knows who she is.

Slate covers her mouth, then her shoulders start shaking.

"Are you laughing?"

"I'm sorry."

"What's so funny?"

"My mother quizzed me about the exact same thing. I told her I didn't think you were choosing a maid of honour and she said that was impossible and asked if we'd had an argument."

Meg sinks onto the bed beside Slate. "Now I see. I should have invited your mother and let her and my mom plan the wedding together."

"Oh, wow. Then I think you'd have a murder on your hands instead of a wedding."

Meg laughs. "And the complete opposite of my ideal wedding."

"Which is?" Slate asks.

"Honestly, I probably would have done it tonight. Around the fire. Toasts with marshmallows." Meg shrugs. "But if things go the way I hope they will tomorrow, it will be pretty close to exactly what I want."

Slate reaches out and squeezes her friend's hand.

"Well, here's to things going the way you hope."

"Deal," Meg says, and the crack of thunder that fills the air feels like an exclamation mark.

Austen

HER PHONE rips her awake in the middle of the night –
the shrill *wee-waw-wee-waw* filling their bedroom with
confusing, reverberating, blaring, siren-like noise that's
completely unnatural.

Oh god, an amber alert. She finds them terribly upset-
ting – worse since Eliot died. They always give only bare
bones information – a child you can tell is vulnerable
from the description. It will be something like, "Brown
hair, green eyes, four years old, wearing running shoes
that light up and a t-shirt with a unicorn on the front."

As if that's not enough, the supplied height and weight
are tiny – usually measured in centimetres and kilograms
barely into double digits.

She can never relax until the alert is called off. To Austen it feels as though Eliot's out there – untethered and uncared-for – until she knows the child's OK.

That's why she turns her phone off at night, so she won't wake up then, unable to sleep, wake Rand, when he needs his sleep because of the long hours he works and the hard physical labour he does.

Except tonight she forgot.

Heart racing, fingers trembling, with no chance for her night vision to kick in, she fumbles for the phone, drops it, hangs over the edge of the bed to retrieve it, feels the blood rushing to her head, slides to the floor with a thump, scrabbles to reach the phone and to turn it over, then struggles to read the glaring words on the dark background.

"What happened? What is it? Where are you?" Rand's voice comes from up high, on the mattress, where normal people are at 1:44 in the morning.

"There's a tornado warning," Austen tells him.

* * *

Rand won't let her get in the car and drive to the barn.

"The horses are fine," he says. "Mac's fine. You put him in the loafing shed yourself."

"But the door's open. He might not have stayed inside."

"The door's open for a reason. So that if it's safer for him to leave, he can. Horses have a one-thousand-pound sense of self-preservation."

"What if Meg and Jared aren't OK?"

"Austen, I'm really sorry to say this, but these tornado warnings usually only go out a few minutes before a tornado hits – sometimes even afterward. There's not much you can do now."

"But ..."

"Why do you think they send the warnings? It definitely isn't so you can leave this old, strong building that's withstood over a hundred years of weather, to go out into the night in your sub-compact car."

"I'd take your truck."

"Austen ..." He slips down beside her, leans against the bed. Lifts the phone from her hands.

"I just can't bear to lose anybody else." She whispers it, as though saying it out loud will make it happen.

Rand slides his arm around her and pulls her head onto his shoulder. "I know. I really do. And I can't bear to lose you."

"You won't."

He kisses her forehead. "Well, I definitely don't plan to tonight. And tomorrow, as soon as the sun's up, we'll drive to the barn together."

"I'll never sleep."

"Let's see." He stands and pulls her to her feet. "Climb under the sheets while I do this ..." He flings the curtains open just as a lightning flash illuminates everything outside for one second ... two seconds ... then darkness takes over again. "Let's watch the show."

Rand's crazy if he thinks she's going to sleep. But she knows he's trying, so she keeps her mouth shut and sits through one, two, three more long lightning flashes and the next thing she knows there's light full in her face, except there's warmth behind it, and she realizes it's the morning sun falling across her cheek.

Meg

RAIN ON the metal roof. Wind buffeting the windows. The firm mattress and soft pillow. The warmth of Jared's body welcome now that the humidity's broken.

Slate's job. Meg's been waiting for this quiet time to think Slate's situation through.

A dress. She wonders if they'll actually find one.

Breakfast. When should she get up to make it if they're trying to catch an early ferry?

A goat. She can't believe Cam got them a goat. Except she also can. She wonders if they're actually as much trouble as everybody says they are.

Her mind flicks from topic to topic. Jared shifts in his sleep and his hand reaches out; he curls his fingers through hers.

Several times she's nearly asleep when a gust of wind and a rattle of rain wakes her again.

Then the noise. Loud, confusing, intrusive. She sits up in bed. "What?" Glances over, but Jared's sound asleep.

It's coming from downstairs.

She slides out of bed and pads across the floor and down the stairs, crossing her arms and rubbing her cool skin. The air's much colder than just a few hours ago.

In the basket on the shelf inside the front door are both their phones. Meg's dark and silent. Jared's quiet now, but with the screen still glowing.

She grabs it up, blinking to clear her eyes. **Special Weather Statement. At 1:42 a.m. Eastern Daylight Time, Environment Canada has issued a tornado warning for this mobile coverage area. Take cover immediately if threatening weather approaches.**

Cam.

Her brother's sleeping in a barn during a tornado warning. She should never have let him. Slate was right – Slate had more common sense than she did.

Just because Cam's her big brother, and he's always been capable, and she's never seen him get himself into a situation he can't get out of, and … a little bit … because he bought her a goat for her wedding, she let him sleep in the hayloft.

Well, she's going to go get him now.

A quick backtrack up the stairs to grab leggings and a hoodie tells her both Jared and Slate are still sound asleep. She eases out the door with Jared's truck keys in her hand and for a flashing second, wonders if she should just head back in.

It's a beautiful night. The air's cool and clean. The moon peeks through scudding clouds. Sure, there's some wind, but it's what would be considered a gentle breeze on this windy island.

Threat, danger, and tornado warnings seem like part of another reality.

Then, in the distance, a split of lightning jags through the sky. A chorus of yips floats through the night air, rising to howls and lifting more goosebumps on Meg's skin than the newly cooled air.

That's it – she's bringing her brother back here.

***

It's clear no tornado touched down anywhere near the barn. The porch light is on at the otherwise-dark farmhouse – empty for a month or so while Jared's mother lives in town to take care of his aunt who just had a knee replacement.

The weathered whitewash and silver roof of the barn are light against the night-filled paddocks and sky.

She approaches the loafing shed but doesn't go in – if the horses are fine she doesn't want to disturb them. A sideways glance shows solid shapes darker than even the darkness they're dozing in. Hooves shift in straw, and the shine of an eye turns in her direction. Nobody's bothered, though. Everything's fine there.

As she walks through the still barn another errant lightning flash backlights her, throwing her shadow in front of her.

She knows this place so well – she spends at least as much time here as in the house – just a few hours ago they were all merrily gathered around the fire a short distance outside the double doors, but it's all different now.

Of course small things scuttle out of sight in all barns, but suddenly now, as it's time to lift her hand to the first rung of the hayloft ladder she's thinking about it. The possibility that a mouse could scamper across her knuckles, that a bat could swoop down from the hatch, the vulnerability of turning her back to the expanse of the barn as she climbs the ladder.

The thing to do would be to call Cam's name, but she hates it when the victim-to-be walks into an unlit space and starts calling things out – "Hello!" "Who's there?" – Meg always squeezes Jared's hand and says, "The killer's there and now he knows where they are!" and she's usually right.

That's why, even though this isn't a murder mystery, she can't bring herself to yell, "Yoo-hoo, Cam!" into the otherwise quiet night.

It's fine.

Reach. Step. Climb.

It's just her barn.

Reach. Step. Climb.

It's actually quite useful when the lightning strikes in the distance since she can see exactly where she's going.

Reach. Step. Climb.

It's the familiar old hayloft where she ate lemon loaf with Jared and fell in love with him.

Reach. Step. Climb.

As always, there's a change in air pressure and temperature, when her head passes from the open air of the barn, through the hatch into the hay-stacked loft. There's a muffled feeling she equates with snug safety.

That's good. The worst is over. She'll just find Cam and … "Aa-a-ah!" Her hand hits something warm and soft, her heart skips several beats, her body goes cold, then rushes hot.

Next comes a nibble on her finger, followed by a bleat, then Cam's voice, "What the hell?"

"The goat!" Meg yells. "It scared me to death. I could have fallen off the ladder!"

"What are you even doing in the hayloft?"

"What's a goat doing in the hayloft?" Meg's followed Cam's voice to find his sleeping bag spread across several hay bales.

He's sitting up, rubbing his eyes. "I don't know. I was asleep."

"Goats don't climb. Please tell me goats don't climb."

"Meg. Why are we talking about the goat? Why are you here at ... what time is it?"

"The tornado warning was at 1:42, so I'm guessing it's around 2:00 now."

"Tornado warning?"

"Yes, that's what I've been trying to tell you. You have to come back to the house."

"Meg. I think if there was a tornado at 1:42, it's missed us."

Meg crosses her arms. "I don't care. I'll never sleep if I leave you here, and it's my wedding tomorrow, sp if Mom comments on the dark circles under my eyes, I'll tell her to talk to you."

"Yeah, OK, I'm not facing Mom tomorrow. I'll come, on one condition."

"What?"

"The goat comes too."

Slate

SHIVERS RUN UP Slate's arm. It's because she's holding Adam's hand again, except this time, instead of dropping it, she's using it as an anchor to pull them closer together to let her stand on her tiptoes and brush her lips against his and ...

Why is her hand wet?

And it's not exactly shivering, or tingling, it's more straight-up tickling in a way that's not quite as sexy as she'd like it to be.

A tiny bleat makes her open one eye in the desperate hope that what she thinks is happening isn't ... except it is. There's a goat nibble-licking her hand.

All goats look quite similar to Slate, but this one is small and is a lovely taupe colour, with a splash of white across its face, very like the goat Cam gave to Meg. So much like, that she's pretty sure it's the same goat.

Having said that, unlike the goat that was handed over last night, this one's wearing a diaper.

Now that she's awake – at least she's pretty sure she is, and that the diapered goat is no figment of a marshmallow-and-lightning infused deep sleep – she becomes aware of voices.

"... how bad?"

"... power out ... barn collapsed ... roof blown off ... car overturned ... row of poplars ..."

"... miracle nobody was killed ..."

It takes Slate a while to process the words spoken in Meg and Jared's voices, broken up by the gurgle of the coffee maker and the hum of the vent hood.

Eventually she strings enough of them together to figure out something's happened. Something not good at all.

She rolls her head sideways and blinks at the clock on a little shelf by the bed. No wonder she's not quite awake.

It's *early*.

Surely this is early even for Meg and Jared to be up.

Slate suspects it has something to do with the bad thing they're talking about. Thinks she should probably get up and ask.

She has a really hard time forcing herself out from under the heavenly quilt, but manages it and yawns into the kitchen. "Hey, what's up?"

"Oh, Slate. Sorry – we didn't mean to wake you."

"You didn't. It was actually the goat that woke me up."

Behind Meg, Jared holds up the coffee pot with his eyebrows raised. She nods. "Yes, please. I really need that, because I thought the goat was wearing a diaper."

"Well, this one isn't potty trained, so you should be glad I had a spare diaper in the truck." Slate turns to face Cam wearing low-slung joggers on bottom and nothing on top other than the little goat tucked in under his arm.

"Are you auditioning for a month in a sexy millennial farmers catalogue?" she asks.

Meg wrinkles her nose. "Are we thinking this is sexy?"

Slate's now completely confused. "Why are you even here?" She asks Cam before turning to Meg. "Didn't you and I have angst over Cam sleeping in the hayloft?"

"My sister's tough love stance crumbled in the face of a tornado."

"A what? Oh … was that what you were talking about?"

Meg nods. "The alert went out at 1:42. I heard it on Jared's phone and I started feeling guilty for leaving my brother sleeping in a hayloft when there was a tornado warning. Not that I thought there would actually be a tornado, but apparently, yes. One touched down and did massive damage in one section on the west side of the island."

"Was that the flipped cars and torn-off roofs?" Slate asks.

Meg nods. "There are bits and pieces of information trickling in on social media. Nobody has the whole story, but there's a meeting at the village hall at 8:00 to get the latest information and try to figure out how everyone can help.

Meg wrinkles her nose. "I'm sorry, that means Jared and I will be abandoning you for a while. But you should treat this place like it's yours. I'll leave my car and you can ride the horses if you want."

"Do the horses need to be ridden?"

"Excuse me?"

"If you don't need me to ride them, I'd rather come with you."

"Oh! No, they're fine on turnout – they were going to have the day off anyway because of ..."

"... your wedding ..." Slate claps her hand over her mouth. "Oh my ... I'm sorry ... I was just in another world ... what's going to ...?"

Meg bites her lip and shakes her head. "One thing at a time. The first thing has to be finding out who needs help ..." as Meg lets the sentence trail off, Slate nods. There are people to be helped and ever since she lost her job she's been afraid she wouldn't have a chance to do that. "What should I wear?"

Meg laughs. "Do you remember when you used to beg me to let you paint my nails before I went to the barn?"

"Are you saying only I would ask what to wear to a disaster?"

"Something like that."

Jared speaks up. "It's a good question. Did you bring a pair of jeans? If so, wear them – or at least not shorts. And you should wear tough boots – paddock boots, or even steel-toed if we can find a pair to fit you."

Slate nods. "Will do." She wants to take Meg aside. Wants to say, *"It's OK if you're secretly freaking out," "You're allowed to be upset that this happened on the day of your wedding," "You can talk to me about it if you want."*

But Jared's pouring their coffee into travel mugs and somebody's phone is ringing, and Meg's telling Cam to put on a shirt and not to bring the goat, and Slate realizes whatever she's going to wear today, it definitely can't be pyjamas.

Better get going.

Lacey

THIS HALL is brimming with memories. A bash for her parents' tenth anniversary – not long before they split up – with a band made up of a bunch of local guys and a pig being roasted on a spit outside.

Then, later, her grandparents' fortieth anniversary – this time with a woman from the church playing the piano, and tables covered with circular sandwiches with mysterious purple, and green, and pink fillings.

She had her first kiss at that party. A red-haired cottager from the city. Exotic because he wore cropped linen pants and sandals that exposed his long, narrow feet. And because his red-headedness was nothing like the gingery streak that ran through certain island families, giving their hair orangey highlights in the sun and bringing out freckles on their tanned faces. No, his hair was auburn – dark with glossy curls – his skin was startlingly white, and his eyes glittered green.

At that time, Lacey couldn't have told anybody the eye colour of any of the guys she grew up with.

The final thing that made him exotic was that he wanted to kiss her. It was exciting and scary. She didn't mind that he was leaving at the end of the summer – it meant she didn't have to face up to the reality of life after that kiss.

She'd had crushes after that, and when she met Fitch she even – sort of – thought she was nursing a broken heart, but now ...

She looks sideways at Fitch, watching the stage, listening to the mayor speaking.

Lacey reaches behind her head and works at a knot in her long hair and wonders why she feels exactly like somebody who was woken up twenty minutes ago with the news of a tornado touch-down and this community meeting, whereas Fitch looks perfect.

Wait, maybe not quite. She can just make out the faintest of pillow creases on his cheek.

Fitch senses her, glances sideways, and smiles like the sun coming out. Reaches out to fold her hand in his and locks his attention back on Mayor Amherst.

Why couldn't it be a boy from here who set her heart, and skin, and senses, alive?

Why couldn't it be somebody else who remembers this hall – yes, for their own family's anniversaries, but also for an endless parade of community events. Music concerts and polling stations, fundraisers for fires, and floods, and illnesses. Gatherings marking the passing of the seasons and the years: late spring strawberry socials, the Canada Day pancake breakfast, the deep-summer fish fries, and the Thanksgiving turkey dinners.

And, of course, like now, as a place to come together when nobody knows exactly what to do, but everybody knows they need to do something.

There's one of those guys sitting one row over from them now. He glances her way, and smiles, and she smiles back and all she can feel is affection that they're both here to help, and happiness for him that the pretty girl sitting next to him – a kindergarten teacher on the mainland, according to social media posts – is going to marry him in a New Year's ceremony.

He doesn't set her heart on fire. Not him, and not anybody else.

She needs Fitch for that.

She squeezes his hand and locks her attention in on the mayor as he hands the microphone to a man she recognizes as the former captain of the ferry. A friend of her dad's, and someone the whole island respects.

"Hey folks," he says. "No doubt somebody more qualified than me will show up at some point, but in the meantime, we've made up some job assignments so we can start getting help where it's needed. This is what I propose ..."

Meg

MEG IS ODDLY HAPPY. Not, of course, for the people whose cars are flipped and barns blown down. Come to think of it, maybe happy's the wrong word.

Grateful.

That's more like it. Her barn is fine. Her animals are safe – all of them – even the new goat.

Her friends are fine. Most of them are here. From where she and Jared stand at the back of the hall she spies Lacey and Fitch sitting in chairs further up. She gets occasional glimpses of a bustling Betsy through the door that leads to the hall's old-fashioned-but-functional galley kitchen.

Slate's slightly to her left, brow furrowed as she scans the crowd. It must be a lot for her; finding herself in this room full of strangers.

Cam, on the other hand, is laughing at something the guy next to him has said and holding a coffee Meg has no idea where he got. In Cam's world nobody's a stranger.

Most importantly Jared's right beside her, fingers threaded through hers. While it's true they live – and to a certain extent, work – together, what with Jared's duties with Rod, and the ever-present needs of the horses, not to mention Meg's more-than-occasional supply teaching shifts, they have less chances than you might think to stand side-by-side like this.

Of course they're supposed to be doing this – standing side-by-side – at this very hall, in about ten hours. Is that even possible? Meg's brain starts to go where she's been trying to keep it from going when something the mayor says catches her attention.

She gives Jared's hand two short, sharp squeezes. "Did he just say the ferry isn't running?"

* * *

They pull into the driveway of the farm they've been sent to and discover a lop-sided game of slow-motion soccer in progress. Lop-sided because one woman, wearing loose pyjama bottoms, an oversized t-shirt, and a backward baseball cap is serving as goalie, standing in a very wide gap in a fence, trying to hold back a couple of dozen animals – real-live soccer balls – with the help of a single defending border collie.

"Are those alpacas?" Slate asks from the backseat.

"I think so," Meg says. "I always get them mixed up with llamas."

Jared taps the assignment sheet they got back at the hall. "I'd say so." Meg picks it up and holds it for Slate to see the directions leading them to Bluebird Lane and their destination of Armstrong Alpacas.

Meg's guessing the pyjama-clad woman is an Armstrong.

They climb out of the truck and walk over to the woman and her dog.

"I'm sorry I can't say hello properly," she says without facing them. "The last time I turned around a bunch of them bolted. My husband helped me herd them back in, but he's gone to see what building materials he can borrow from the neighbours, so it's just Luna and me."

"Not anymore," Jared says. "We're here to help now."

In that moment, something floods through Meg. A memory – a series of memories of all the times she's been able to count on Jared – Jared finding Salem after she jumped clear of her paddock. Jared walking Jessie safely through her colic. Jared calming both her and Jessie when the little mare was belly-deep in barbed wire.

She sees how his calm kindness reassures this woman. How she takes a deep breath, then rolls her shoulders back and nods and says, "Thank you."

As Jared says, "Slate, you can help stand guard, and Meg, most of the fenceposts look OK; let's see how many boards we can salvage and start getting this fence back up," Meg can see how he'll always be a pillar of strength. How it's his gift to offer.

There's no time to dwell on that feeling – they have a fence to reassemble – but she lets it percolate in the back of her mind as they walk along the downed fence line and separate the reusable lengths of board from the ones the tornado's turned to kindling.

She wants to be able to count on Jared for the rest of her life. She wants him to count on her. She thought they had that anyway so the actual wedding ceremony wasn't that important.

She was wrong.

It *is* important. She wants it. She knew how much in the moment she realized that, yes, the mayor had said the ferry wasn't running. It cemented the fears she'd been trying to keep at bay since waking up. No ferry means no rings, no dress, no guests from off the island – including Jared's mom. No deliveries – some of which were probably needed for their meal.

It also, of course, has a much bigger meaning. It means no normalcy for anyone on this island. Disruption of many, many plans. Uncertainty and anxiety for people with medical conditions and other pressing needs.

It means there are much bigger problems than her wedding ceremony being postponed.

It still hurts, though.

An alpaca rushes her, and she picks up a fence board and uses it like a lunging whip to guide the animal back.

Stop getting ahead of yourself. This is how the day has to go. One fence board at a time. One alpaca at a time. One issue at a time. *Worry about things when they're right in front of you.*

There's another alpaca right in front of her.

Austen

BY THE TIME they get to the hall, cars and trucks are pouring out onto the road.

"I can't believe I slept so late," Austen says. "I can't believe you let me."

"It was better than the alternative," Rand says, and she can't argue with him.

Better than the possible alternative version of last night in which she didn't fall asleep but instead paced the floor, fretting about her horse, worrying about Meg, and Jared, and all their other friends on the island.

Also, better than almost every single night in the last several months. There were a couple of nights right after Eliot died – after her sister's starved body literally shut down one organ at a time – when Austen slept right through. She thinks it was the shock. Her body literally stepping in to shut her brain down so she wouldn't have to face the unbelievable fact that even with the best medical help available, even in a hospital, even with the fierce love of her family surrounding her, Austen's oh-so-funny, crazily sarcastic, much-too-young sister, had died.

After that early reprieve, Austen hasn't slept through the night once. Even when she's not actively sad, she's unsettled.

Last night, though ... after the emergency warning, at any rate, she was completely out. So much so that there's still a slight fog lingering with her, but not in a bad way.

It's actually kind of a delicious feeling. Like she went somewhere really nice while she slept and tendrils of it still cling to her.

Even though they slept much later than she would have chosen to, she can't be bothered by it. She feels nothing could bother her today.

When she sipped the coffee Rand put in a travel mug for her, it was just the right temperature, with the exact perfect amount of milk in it.

When they drove by Meg's barn, the sun was glinting off the metal roof and Mac was out in the field. He lifted his head, and kicked up his heels, and ran beside the truck along the fence line.

And even now – sure, they've missed the meeting, and normally that would really bother her, but Austen just shrugs and texts Meg and within a minute a text pings back containing an address.

"Bluebird Lane?" she asks Rand.

"I know it," he says.

Of course he does. It's that kind of morning.

"I should buy a lottery ticket," Austen says, and Rand glances across at her and smiles, and she's filled with a surge of love so strong it brings tears to her eyes.

How nice to feel again and how nice that her first real feeling in months is love.

Her spirits are tested when they turn into the driveway of Armstrong Alpacas.

On one side of the drive Meg holds a board in place against a post while Jared drives screws into it. Beside them Meg's friend Slate – the one who scared Austen half out of her wits yesterday when she knocked on her car window – along with another woman and a dog guard a gap in the fence.

It's what's on the other side of the driveway that widens Austen's eyes. Behind a compact board and batten farmhouse is what looks like a barn that was dropped from a great height ... or, she guesses, hit by a tornado.

The reason it looks like a barn is because it's the right general shape and size for a barn and it contains barn-like materials. Lots of wood, metal which was probably a roof, but none of it with any structure to it. As though the insides gave up and everything just fell where it could.

Rand parks next to Jared's truck and she slips out, facing the blown-in barn; shielding her eyes against the bright sun.

"You OK?" When she turns to face Rand, she finds his brow creased with worry. His familiar shape, and smell, and voice rekindle that dreamy feeling she's had all morning, and she smiles at him.

"Yeah, just thinking what a good thing it is that I never took your new drill out of the car."

Slate

This is what her parents don't understand. This need she has – this compulsion – to be helpful.

She's heard of families where it runs deep – where everybody is in the military, or a first responder, or where there's an abundance of nurses or teachers.

That is not Slate's family. Her dad does something in finance that her mom's never been able to explain (something about backwardation?). Her mom only started working later in life, as an event planner. Not charity events, though. Mostly celebrations for older, wealthy people – anniversaries, or these big annual bashes thrown to keep business contacts close and pay back a years' worth of entertaining debts in one, extravagant go.

"It's completely meaningless," Slate complained to her sister, who asked, "What harm does it do?"

"The helium balloons they release end up in the Great Lakes, and that gender reveal party she did for Miranda Baxby's granddaughter – that was just toxic."

"Hmm, yeah, well you can criticize our parents all you like, but you took the ponies and the horses. You were happy to get the Golf when you turned sixteen. And last Christmas – did you return those Manitobah Mukluks Mom gave you?"

Slate did take the horses, and all that came with them, and she did accept the dolphin grey Golf. She did her high school volunteer hours as the greeter in the VIP tent for a charity polo match sponsored by her dad's firm – she actually drank champagne while getting volunteer hours.

Looking back now, it embarrasses her.

She woke up to her privilege very suddenly and painfully when she fell for a charity-and-volunteer superstar at university.

Where Slate's parents were well-off, this guy's family was full-on wealthy. Old money. He had to fight with his dad to fire the bodyguard who had come to campus with him.

He would occasionally give his residence room to homeless people for the night, while he slept on whatever floor he could find. One night the floor was Slate's.

She fell in love – hard – and the next time she was very drunk she told him so and he said, "Sorry. I mean, we can sleep together if you like, but I don't date cosseted daddy's girls who grew up in four-bedroom houses in nice neighbourhoods."

She was mortified he could peg her without even really knowing her, and she was heart-broken – at least for long enough to switch her major from business to sociology and then go onto law school.

Her dad was fine with the change at first – "We could use a corporate lawyer in the family" – but when she articled in the legal aid office, then joined the university-run pro bono clinic, he'd shaken his head. "Why? It's just as easy to enjoy a well-paying job as one that pays you minimum wage."

But was it? Not for Slate.

"I don't earn minimum wage," she'd protested, but it wasn't that far off – especially after the government's recent minimum wage hikes. Close enough, that when her mom gave her those lovely boots, she couldn't bring herself to return them.

She was doing good at work, she reasoned. She helped a working single mother fight her landlord to keep her apartment. That made up for the boots.

But what about now? What good was she doing? Just last night her dad emailed her a posting for in-house legal counsel at his firm.

No way. She can't do it. She can't cave. But the fear that she *might* is real.

Which is why now, under the bright-but-cool October sun, she's never been so happy to fetch and carry.

To cart away the broken fence boards Jared deems beyond fixing and to get him more screws from his toolbox. To go into the small-but-sweet farmhouse kitchen and put on a twelve-cup pot of coffee.

To look everywhere on the property until she comes up with enough lengths of rope to span the remaining space between the now-repaired portion of the fence and the part that never came down.

The farm owner, released from her alpaca guard duty, looks like she's going to collapse – like the only thing keeping her on her feet was the requirement to keep the animals contained.

The vagueness of her eyes worries Slate. She's seen it before in clients who come to the clinic with a legitimate case, but still with lots of work ahead to win it. There are always some who just shake their heads, "I'm tired. I can't keep doing this."

Slate loves this little farm. The board-and-batten farmhouse with its restful wrap-around porch. The view over a sparkling bay of the St. Lawrence. The loyal border collie. The sweet-and-ditsy-looking alpacas who have now moved en masse away from the temporarily repaired break in the fence.

"Of course they have," the woman says. "They wouldn't stay away when it was just me and Luna, but now they have no interest in this part of the field at all."

The laugh she gives is weak, but at least it *is* a laugh. In Slate's experience, that's a good sign – where there's laughter, there's life.

"Come on," Slate tells her. "I think somebody's just brought muffins and pastries from the bakery and there's more coffee."

The woman's gaze wanders to the collapsed barn.

"That's what we all have to talk about now," Slate encourages her. "How to get your barn back up."

The woman blinks, and a slow tear rolls down her face. Slate doesn't want her to be sad, but she does feel the stirrings of a purpose.

Surely there will be insurance forms to fill out. Probably government assistance to apply for. Slate's good at those things. She can chivvy the woman through them. They can go through everything together once the barn meeting's over.

Which is why she's irritated to hear a voice say, "Alanna? It's OK. I'm here now," and to have the woman say, "Oh!" and turn away toward the interloper.

Meg

ONE THING AT A TIME – that was the plan, right? There continue to be things right in front of Meg ... in front of all of them.

A tree across the end of the driveway blocking vehicle access to the caved-in barn.

A dog running back and forth, back and forth across her path until she follows him to a spot at the edge of the fallen barn where a pitiful meowing comes from under a heap of debris. Meg lifts a panel of metal roofing and a cat shoots past her without a backward glance.

Another dog – one she's already met; the border collie named Luna – making her glance up to see his owner standing off to the side staring at the downed barn.

The woman's changed out of pyjamas now and the baseball cap she's wearing fits her head and is turned around the proper way with a ponytail pulled through the opening in the back. She looks younger – closer to "girl" than "woman." Meg narrows her eyes. "Alanna? Alanna Turlington? Is that you?"

Alanna turns. As she smiles most of the tension leaves her face. "I thought your voice was familiar when you arrived. It's amazing to see you Meg."

"This is your place?"

Now there's pride on Alanna's face, too. "It is now. The farm was in my husband, Steve's, family as a dairy farm. We bought it from his uncle to raise alpacas, among other things. We're building a greenhouse this spring to grow cut flowers." Her face falls. "*Were* building a greenhouse, that is. Now, I guess we have other priorities."

Meg steps to Alanna's side and puts one arm around the girl while the border collie nudges her nose into Meg's free hand. "I know it's a lot to take in," she says. "But we're all going to do our best to help you get sorted out. And, big picture, Alanna – this is amazing. I keep up with what Adam's doing, but I had no idea you'd settled here."

She nods. "Of course I'm really happy to be here. This is just – like you say – a lot." She smiles again. "But I'm grateful to all these people who have showed up, and your friend who came with you ..."

"Slate?"

"Yes. Slate. She's already started sending messages and filling out insurance forms."

Meg laughs. "Slate is the best person I can imagine to help with that. You'll see – you'll have the best new barn imaginable once Slate talks to those insurance people."

"Meg? Is that you, Meg?" In response to the voice calling her from near the house, Meg turns and shades her eyes against the strong morning sun. "Whoa, speaking of all the people here, that's my mother." She gives Alanna's shoulder a final squeeze. "I'd better go talk to her. I'll see you later."

Meg's taken two steps toward her mother when Alanna calls, "Oh, by the way, Adam's back here for a few days."

Meg stops. "Is he?"

"Yes. He came back for ..."

Meg claps her hand over her mouth. "Oh, my goodness, of course. Your grandfather's funeral. I was so sad to hear he died." She shakes her head. "You *have* been through a lot, Alanna." She pauses, then adds. "Well, thank you for telling me. You should ..."

She was going to say, "Come to my wedding and bring him," because, why not? Anything held at the hall is pretty much a community affair anyway, and Meg loved her time coaching Alanna, and she holds absolutely no hard feelings toward Adam ... except ... the wedding. Will there be one? Instead she says, "You should tell him I'm here if you see him."

Then she heads off to her waiting mother where she's pretty sure the wedding – and whether it's happening – is going to be a topic of conversation.

***

Meg owes Cam.

Meg will never make another disparaging remark about the goat. Meg will sew up the rip in Cam's favourite vintage Rush t-shirt he's wearing today even though she hates both Rush's music and the t-shirt. Meg will tell Cam to plan a weekend away with Lynsey and she'll go to Lake Placid and look after their animals.

None of this seems too much when her brother swoops in and puts his arm around their mother's shoulders and steers her away toward the bakery table all while throwing a wink over his shoulder in her direction.

I love you, she mouths.

I know, he replies.

Austen

"SHOW ME AGAIN how to change the battery pack." Rand says.

Austen looks up at him. "I honestly don't think I'm going to need the drill. I'm on clean-up crew."

Rand nods. "A good drill is essential for clean-up crew – do you know how many of those boards have screws that need to be taken out of them? You'll definitely use up your battery so please show me how to change the pack."

Austen sighs, releases the current battery pack and slides the spare one into place with a final whack for good measure. She raises her eyebrows. "Good?"

"Not bad," Rand says, but you forgot the most important thing."

Austen presses the trigger and the drill whines to life. "Looks good to me."

Rand shakes his head. "Oh, Austen. Austen, Austen." Jared's walking by and he grabs at his shirt sleeve. "Can you please tell Austen which critical step she's missed in the battery swap process?"

Jared grins, teeth flashing in the sunlight. He leans in and whispers in Austen's ear, "He wants you to put the old battery on the charging station."

She looks at Rand. "Seriously?"

"A battery's no good if it isn't charged."

"That's not part of the battery changing process."

"It's the lynchpin of the battery changing process."

Rand's smiling, and Jared's smiling, and Austen's heart is light. and her face hurts because it's out of smiling practice. These are the things you don't even know you're missing until they're back. Ribbing, and banter, and levity. She scoops up the drill and the spare battery pack. "I'm going to conduct a survey to see how many people agree with you."

Rand crosses his arms. "Fine, as long as you put the battery on the charger first."

On Austen's first try the battery won't fit. Lacey reaches over, lifts it, turns it, and settles it successfully on the charger. "Don't you tell me about the importance of charging drill batteries, too ..." Austen says.

"OK, I won't. How about you tell me how my cousin is."

Austen furrows her brow. "Your cousin … oh! Jared. Fine, other than being annoyingly supportive of Rand. Why wouldn't he be?"

"Well, for one thing, his wedding isn't going to happen, and for another thing, Adam's here."

Austen freezes, stares at Lacey, and covers her mouth with her hand.

Lacey leans in. "Austen? Are you OK? You look like you're going to faint."

Austen shakes her head. "I'm just realizing what a truly self-absorbed, clueless person I am."

"What do you mean?"

"I woke up happy today. For the first time in I can't remember how long. I've been bubbling along in my own world, and … the wedding … I just never thought about it. I mean, I thought it would be different than we expected, but I didn't think …" She looks at Lacey. "I'm an idiot. I took the wedding for granted. Do I take Meg for granted? I feel like I've spent the last few months being impossible and not thinking of other people because I'm so wrapped up in my own grief, but now, clearly, as soon as I'm happy I don't think of other people either."

"Wow," Lacey says.

"Wow, what?"

"Wow, you need to snap out of it, Austen. You're happy! That's awesome. You deserve it. And as to taking

Meg and Jared for granted – we all do. It's part of what makes them them. They're rock solid, and they're there for us, and the horses, and even if this wedding doesn't happen today – which, I'm sorry, Austen, but I don't see how it can – they'll figure it out. If you just assume they're fine, that's because we all do, and because they will be."

Austen blinks a couple of times. "You're right, I guess."

Lacey nods. "Of course I'm right."

"OK, then I do have another question."

"Which is?"

"Who's Adam?"

Meg

THE NEARLY-having-to-talk-to-her-mom moment has made Meg realize she definitely has to talk to Jared.

After all, she should be in a changing room striking unnatural poses in front of unrealistically angled mirrors wearing a dress that's too pretty for her comfy cotton underwear, with Slate outside the door encouraging, "Show me!"

They should be swinging by the jeweler's to pick up the sized-and-cleaned rings.

Lacey and Austen should be checking in to say the horses are fed, and the barn's clean, and everything's under control.

Rand, and Fitch, and Cam should be with Jared, pretending to fish (even though none of them like fishing) because that's a bonding thing to do on your wedding morning, and because Rand's Uncle Kurt offered to take them out in his big fishing boat.

Betsy should be double- and triple-checking the food all socked away in the functional-if-not-pretty kitchen at the hall, and Jared's mom should have made her way over – leaving his aunt in the temporary care of her next-door neighbour for the day – so she can "help" Meg's mom set the tables in the hall ... which really means Jared's good-natured mother treating all Meg's control-loving mother's commands as great "suggestions" and going along with all of them.

As she scans the site, looking for Jared, Meg sees all these people doing very different jobs. Lacey and Austen are carrying bits of splintered boards to a burn pile.

She catches sight of Slate on the porch, phone to her ear, scribbling notes on a pad of paper with her free hand.

Betsy is bustling back and forth between the house and the food table with arms full of baking, and Meg even spots her mom, wearing an apron – will wonders never cease? – filling coffee cups for volunteers.

Having redirected their mother, Cam's freed himself to operate a chainsaw – Meg doesn't stick around to watch that – and Fitch and Rand are both by the edge of the fallen barn in a group of people nodding along as a man points to different areas while he talks to them.

As to what Meg and Jared should be doing – well, they should be meeting the minister of the church affiliated with the community hall in ... Meg glances at her watch ... oh, gosh, not that many hours. Which is how she knows there's no way the wedding can happen.

There's far too much work to do here, and there's no ferry to transport dresses, or rings, or Jared's mother, and all these people – a large number of whom would have been at the hall – are here, working hard, and they're going to be starving after their long day. It's island tradition to feed volunteers in cases like this, and the no-ferry situation means no bringing over any extra food.

"Oh! Jared! I found you!" Meg spots him reaching into the back of a truck to take a couple of two-by-fours. She pauses long enough to register that it's Adam handing them out, and thinks they've come a long way from the days when somebody would have gotten punched if Jared and Adam were this close.

"Adam," she nods and smiles, then says, "I just need to borrow Jared for a minute."

She takes one end of the two-by-fours. "Where are we heading with these?" she asks.

"Follow me," he says and she thinks, *Yes. OK. Of course.* Then she says it, "Nothing I'd rather do." And even though they're not anywhere close to the construction site yet, the boards stop moving. Jared sets his end down and walks back to her. He lifts the end she's carrying and lies them down as well. Then he puts a hand on each of her shoulders and pulls her tight to him. He slides one hand into her hair, while the other wraps across her back. She lays her head against his chest. She knows exactly what's going on. She doesn't need to ask, and she doesn't want to talk about it just yet.

She doesn't want to do anything but stand, and hug, and be hugged.

Finally, though, he pulls back and looks at her and says, "You know I want this to happen, right? You know that?"

She nods. "But ..."

"But ..."

"Your mom can't get over."

"And what's happening here is much more urgent."

"I know."

"I know."

She bites her lip.

He takes a shaky breath.

"Good can still come out of it," she says.

"I was thinking that, but I wasn't sure what you'd think."

"I think we have all the food at the hall, and all these hard-working people here."

"And the hall will keep. Our vows will keep."

"... but the food won't."

"... so we should serve it up."

Meg nods. "We should. And it will be a great night. A different great night than we expected but still great."

"I love you," Jared says.

"I love you," Meg says. "Also ..."

"Also, what?"

"Well, full disclosure, I don't have a wedding dress."

"You don't ... how did that happen? Or not happen?" Jared shakes his head. "Forget it. This way you have time to get one." He grins. "I guess it was meant to be."

"Something was meant to be." Meg flings her arms around him and pulls him close and whispers in his ear. "Don't let me go."

"As if I would. This is just a tiny setback."

"No, I mean literally, don't let me go. My mom's looking around and I suspect it's for me."

CHAPTER TWENTY-ONE

Slate

SHE'S AFRAID of seeing Adam, and she's afraid not to.

She can't imagine never seeing him again. For a brief moment yesterday, it was like everything in her opened up. All those closed-in parts of her that normally say, *"You're stronger on your own,"* and *"Don't mistake lust for love,"* and *"Love doesn't happen at first sight,"* – they all dropped away.

She thought, *"I can be in love and still be strong,"* and *"What's wrong with a little lust?"* and *"Meg loved Jared at pretty close to first sight and they're getting married now."* Except, of course, they're not, are they?

She knew. Of course, anyone who thought about it knew, but they make it official now, as everybody takes a break for what passes for lunch. A band of hungry people grouped around loaves of bread surrounded by what must be every jar of peanut butter from the general store, and a bunch of locally made honeys and jams which Slate's discovered are delicious, but which aren't quite filling the void after a morning of lifting and carrying. And considering she spent half that morning on the phone, she can only imagine how hungry the full-time manual labourers are.

Jared clears his throat, then climbs the porch stairs and says, "Meg and I would like to make sure everyone gets a proper full-on meal after all this hard work, so we're inviting you to dinner at the hall at the end of the day."

Everyone who was already invited to the wedding pauses to let his words sink in, but all the others smile, and nod, and somebody claps, so she starts clapping, too. Then Lacey, and Austen, and Betsy join in and soon everybody's applauding – even Meg's mom.

At first Slate's surprised by how well Mrs. Traherne is taking it, but as she watches her clap, it all makes sense.

This gives Meg's mother another chance to pitch for a wedding at the country club, or the Fairmont Hotel downtown in the city, or maybe in the magazine-worthy atrium of the National Nature Museum.

Slate imagines she's quickly figured out the delay's nothing to be ashamed of – nothing she needs to hide from the ladies in her book club, since after all, it was caused by an act of god – and now a whole new world of formal wedding planning is open in front of her.

She makes a mental note to warn Meg, just in case it hasn't already occurred to her. It's as she's glancing around to find her friend that her eyes fall on Adam.

Oh, wow. That's confirmed it – yesterday was no fluke.

Her insides twist up the way she can't remember them doing since she was nine and rode the Zipper at the Carp Fair even though Meg shook her head and said, "No way – that thing will make you throw up," then watched from the ground.

The difference is, this time there are other feelings accompanying the up and down of her stomach. There's her heart, feeling like it's trying to swell its way out of her chest, and there's the smile so wide it pushes her cheeks up to form creases underneath her eyes. Washing over all of these is an immense overall lightness in every part of her, like when you've hyperventilated until you're a bit oxygen starved and all your limbs feel slightly detached and somewhat floaty and your brain is simultaneously taking in way too much information at once and not processing any of it.

That's how Adam makes her feel.

And the crazy thing is, from the look on his face, she thinks he feels that way about her, too.

"Hi again," he says.

"Hi again."

See? They're both reduced to inane, meaningless greetings because their rational brains are no longer working. Slate's sure that's a sign of love.

"I'm glad I can say hi to you. I was afraid I wouldn't see you again. That you'd do your bridesmaidly duties and get up in the morning and leave."

"What would you have done?" Slate asks.

"What do you mean?"

"If that had happened. If there hadn't been a tornado and I was busy all day helping Meg, and I went to the wedding, then in the morning I left – what would you have done?"

Normally Slate would be far too reticent to ask such a direct question, but she's blaming love for this, too – she just can't see any reason to put all her cards on the table. She needs to know, would he have asked Meg for her number?

He runs his hand through the flop-over of hair that covers his forehead – that she already loves – and she holds her breath in case he says something like, "I would have regretted it for the rest of my life."

Because, sure, that sounds romantic, but it indicates a complete willingness to let her go. That's one thing that made her really good at her old job; she never let things go. She won a lot of cases for her clients, not because she was better, or smarter, but because she kept her eye on the prize and didn't give up.

I mean, look, she's standing here now, in front of him because she came to this clean-up with Meg. Yes, partly that was to help, and partly to support Meg on this day that definitely isn't turning out the way her best friend thought it would, but, as with so many other things in life, even seemingly unselfish acts have something in it for the person doing them, and in Slate's case she knew, back when Meg said she could stay at the barn and ride the horses, that there would be no way she'd see Adam there.

Which is why she's standing here in front of him, waiting and thinking, *Please don't let me down.*

"It wouldn't have come to that," he says.

"Oh, really? How's that?"

"I had a plan."

"What plan was that?"

"I was going to crash the wedding."

"You were!" The words bubble out of her with a giggle behind them. "Really? You were?"

He nods. "I watched The Wedding Crashers last night."

"Excuse me?"

"On Netflix." He shrugs. "I'm a journalist. I like to be prepared. You know, do research. And there aren't many legitimate sources of wedding crashing resources."

"… so you went with a movie from the early 2000s?"

"What can I say? I like Owen Wilson."

Slate crosses her arms. "I thought this was about being prepared."

"Oh, it was."

Slate bites her lip, "Is this something you do regularly?"

"Only for really important things."

"Like?"

"Like, I binge-watched The Newsroom before my interview with the Gazette. And, when I got sent to cover the Junos – when The Tragically Hip were playing – I listened to their entire discography on repeat for a week."

Slate interrupts. "That's not preparation – that's just good musical taste."

Adam grins. "Oh, good. You like The Hip – that's an important thing to establish up front."

"I also like to be prepared." She hesitates. "I'm a lawyer. Was. Am. I'm between jobs right now." It hurts to say it, but she's glad she did.

"So, we both like The Hip, and we both like to be prepared." Adam tilts his head and looks at her, "… which are both important, but they don't mean much if …"

"If what?"

He steps closer. "If ..."

Slate's eyes are locked on his now. All that heady happiness is still there, but now there's a flush filling her body too. Despite that humidity breaking last night, she's hotter now than she was yesterday.

"They don't mean much if ..." she can hardly find the breath to get the words out.

He exhales – a quick, short breath that tells her he's getting ready. He's going to lean in. He's going to kiss her and she's going to let him.

They're going to kiss, and it's going to be amazing, and it will be the final, necessary ingredient in the list of liking The Hip, and being prepared – having scorching chemistry.

"Has anyone seen Slate?" Meg's ultra-familiar voice cuts through the general background noise of distant hammering, and the Bobcat someone's brought to help with the clear-up, and the calling back and forth between Betsy, and Meg's mom, and the rest of the food crew.

"The friend I brought? Pretty. Dark hair and eyes. Helping Alanna with the insurance claim?"

Slate gulps and the being-sick-on-the-Zipper feeling is back, except with the nice things stripped away from it, and she says, "I should go!" and whirls away before

Adam's warm eyes and sunshine-filled smile, and even, white teeth can stop her.

As she taps Meg on the shoulder, Slate thinks, *Nothing else means much if I don't have the guts to tell my best friend I've fallen for her ex.*

Lacey

SOMETIME back around three this morning Fitch circled his arms around Lacey's ribs and mumbled, "Whoa girl, stop tossing and turning."

If only it was that easy. Lacey's sleep continued to be broken up by thoughts of how little time was left before they had to leave again. To be honest, she was almost relieved when Meg, and Jared, and Slate showed up on their doorstep early this morning to make sure they all knew about the tornado and the meeting at the hall.

Of course the tornado was a disaster – terrible for Alanna, and her husband, and others with property damage – but helping with the clean-up has distracted Lacey. Given her a reason to put on a cheerful face.

Kept her too busy to count the days – even hours – before they have to pack up and go.

Hours which, of course, she should be enjoying to the max – not frittering away by worrying about leaving, but she can't help it.

Especially now that she knows Meg and Jared's wedding won't happen today. The chances of her being able to get all the way back here for another weekend anytime soon, are tiny, and the thought of everyone gathering around to witness her cousin's wedding without her is … hard to bear.

She spots Austen off to the side of the site, waving her over. Austen points to a pile of lumber to her right, and a tray of screws to her left. "I'm taking screws out of boards so they can be used again," she tells Lacey. "Could you carry these boards over to the lumber area so they know they're available?"

Lacey hefts several lengths of wood, but they're not enough of a distraction to keep her from dwelling on the knowledge that this is what it's going to be like going forward – missing out on important events. Not being able to come home for all the holidays she'd like to. As beautiful and amazing as Nova Scotia is, it's far from home.

A board starts to slide and she pauses to hitch it back into line with the others.

Lacey knows Nova Scotia is good neutral territory for her and Fitch, and they've had some fantastic times there, and made solid memories, but rather than making things better for her, this quick trip home has revved her homesickness up to a new level.

She drops the boards next to a pile of new lumber and straightens to face a familiar woman holding a clipboard.

Mrs. Carruthers. Lacey's grade one teacher. "Well, Lacey Strickland, as I live and breathe – how long are you home?"

It takes all Lacey's willpower to smile and say, "Oh, for a few days," instead of snapping, "That's the last thing I want to think about!"

She turns away to get another load from Austen – at least Austen doesn't bug her – and nearly runs into Alanna. She falls into step with Lacey, chattering away, "I'm completely overwhelmed by everyone's support and it's such an extra bonus to see you again after all these years, and who would have ever thought I'd be the one who'd end up living here and you'd be the one in Nova Scotia ... you remember Adam moved to Halifax for school?"

It's the only thing that saves Lacey from saying something possibly nasty and likely unforgiveable to Alanna. She nods. "Tell me about your brother. What's he doing here?"

They're both picking up boards from Austen's pile, but that doesn't silence Alanna. "Oh, our grandfather died, you might remember him – he used to run the Ellicott ferry. The funeral is tomorrow – well it's supposed to be tomorrow. We were close to him. He taught Adam to sail, so of course he came back for the funeral, but he'll need to leave again soon."

Just like me. She wonders if Adam wishes he could stick around longer.

Not that it matters. Her misery doesn't love company. It just wants to be momentarily soothed away by Fitch.

And that's the final thing dragging her down. She can't find him anywhere.

A guy from high school has started following her around. Making what he no doubt thinks are funny jokes.

"Couldn't stay away from me any longer, huh Lace?"

Then, with a wink. "Don't worry, the next place they build on this island can be for you and me."

And, finally, when she pulls off her paddock boot to shake out a sharp stone lodged inside. "There she goes – on her way to being barefoot and pregnant, just the way I like her."

Lacey's momentarily stunned, but Austen on the hunt for more screw-filled boards overhears. "I don't know who you are, but that's a completely inappropriate thing to say, not only to Lacey, but to any woman."

Lacey enjoys seeing his mouth drop open, and she enjoys it even more when Austen says, "Go on then, pick up your bottom lip and go somewhere you can be helpful."

As they watch his retreating back, Austen turns to her. "I suppose it's a bit late now, but it just occurred to me he might be a friend of yours. If so, I apologize. It's just ..." She stretches, throws her head back, and turns her face to the sun before looking at Lacey again. "Now that I have my mojo back I'm afraid it's kind of flooding through me."

Lacey laughs. "No need to apologize – he's no friend of mine. And I'm glad about your mojo."

She's not just glad – she's jealous. Lacey could use a little of what Austen's got. In the absence of that, she goes looking for Fitch, but she can't find him anywhere.

There's no other way to look at it – this day's turning out really shitty, which sucks considering every time she slows down she can hear the ticking of the clock in her head counting down the time she has left before she leaves.

Meg

MEG'S REACHING for the door handle of her little car when he calls her name. She pauses and lifts her hand to her brow to block the already-shortening rays of the afternoon sun. "Adam, hey."

That hair, as blond as ever, still in the same slightly shaggy style as in his student days. Which makes sense. He's a print journalist – no need to spiff himself up for the camera. Not that he doesn't look good. He does – just not to Meg.

"I heard about your wedding," Adam says. "Congratulations."

"Yes, and I heard about your grandfather. I'm really sorry. He was special."

"I'm sorry, too." He opens his arms wide. "About all this, pushing your wedding back. Maybe I shouldn't have even brought it up."

Meg laughs. "Hopefully you don't think I'm that touchy. I know you only mean the best."

"I'm glad to hear you say that. I wasn't sure where we stood."

Meg smiles. "Adam, come on, I subscribe to your feed at the Gazette."

"You do?"

"Of course. You're a good writer. I like reading your work. I like knowing you're doing well."

He pushes a tumble of hair away from his eyes. "Does that mean no hard feelings?"

"Only good feelings." She reaches back toward the handle, then pauses. "In fact ..."

"In fact, what?"

"Oh ... maybe you think it's a hollow gesture, but when Alanna told me you were back here, my first instinct was to tell her to invite you to the wedding. Which, of course, isn't happening now, so it's not much of an invitation." She arches her eyebrows. "But if you happen to be here when we reschedule it, I hope you'll come."

Adam thumps his chest. "Not a hollow gesture. Not at all. In fact ..."

Now it's Meg's turn to ask, "In fact, what?"

Before he can answer, somebody calls out, "Meg!"

Both Meg and Adam turn to face Austen who's running, hand pressed to her chest, panting. "I was afraid I wouldn't catch you."

"Well, you can thank Adam. I've been chatting with him."

He nods. "Yes, but I should go. With all these strangers helping my sister I'll be in big trouble if I don't pull my weight."

"You were going to say something, though," Meg prompts.

He waves his hand. "It's not important. To be honest, it's probably nothing."

"If you're sure ..."

"I'm sure I need a ride," Austen says.

"Hop in," Meg says, and when they're both in the car she asks, "Why am I so lucky to have your company?"

"I was told in no uncertain terms that they have more people than they need on clean-up duty here, and that you were on your way to the hall to get the dinner ready. There really isn't that long before there are a pack of hungry volunteers looking for a hot meal."

"In other words, we'd better get going," Meg says, and puts the car in drive.

***

Meg parks the car on the main street. "Betsy's already at the hall. She texted and asked us to swing by the pub to pick up some extra cutlery, then go by the general store to buy all the Oreo cookies they have."

"Oreo cookies?"

Meg shrugs. "The minute this stopped being my wedding dinner I decided to adopt an 'ours not to reason why,' mindset. I might have no idea what Betsy's going to do with all those Oreos, but I'm sure it will be delicious."

"I like that," Austen says.

"You like Oreos?"

"No. I mean, yes – Oreo cookie ice cream is something special and we could never have it when Eliot was alive because she liked it too much. She'd be furious if anyone bought good ice cream – say we were messing with her, trying to tempt her. So we could only have crappy ice cream."

They push into the pub and lean up on the bar. "What's crappy ice cream?" Meg asks.

Austen holds up her hand, ticking off on her fingers, "Tiger Tail. Spumoni – actually offensive. Neapolitan – not so much crappy as incredibly boring. Rum raisin – only eaten by people over age seventy. Except our family. Oh, and Lavender Basil – I mean, seriously, you might as well eat grass clippings."

A girl with two braids and freckles smattered across her cheeks, pushes two bags clinking with cutlery across the bar. "I'm with you, girl. The chef wanted to make bacon ice cream. I told him he was forbidden from ruining two otherwise perfect foods."

Meg and Austen turn away, each carrying a bag. "So, you can have Oreo ice cream now?" Meg asks.

Austen nods. "I guess. It's hard to even think about it though."

"Why?"

"It feels like I'm finding a silver lining in my sister's death."

Meg chews on her lip. "I see what you're saying, but that's not how it looks to me."

"How does it look?"

"It looks like a terrible, difficult, life-changing thing happened to you, and being able to find things that make you happy is the only way to keep moving."

"Hmm ... well that kind of takes us full circle back to what I was saying before. I like that you're willing to go along with whatever Betsy has planned, and assume the best will come from it. Especially considering you have every reason to be bitter."

They're back at the car, and Meg pops the trunk open to let them sling the cutlery in before continuing to the store. "It's funny you say that, because with everything going on I don't think it's even fully registered that we're postponing the wedding." She sighs. "I'm worried I'm going to wake up tomorrow and it's all going to hit me."

"Well, if you do, call me and we'll go for a ride."

"Is that the universal prescription for low spirits?"

Austen hesitates. "It helps, for sure, but ..."

"But what?"

"I don't know what I would have done without Mac all this time – I would have been much worse off – but I also don't know why I woke up this morning and everything felt different. I was itching to do all this work I've been putting off for the business. I could visualize the spreadsheets, and how I'll organize everything. I've meant to do it for ages, and now I can't wait to get started."

Meg laughs. "You definitely need to seize the day on that one, because I'm pretty sure the motivation to do spreadsheets is a fleeting thing."

"There was also ..."

"What?"

"You know that old wooden bed frame Rand brought home from the job he did in the spring?"

"The one that's been leaning against the wall downstairs in the barn ever since I can remember?"

Austen nods. "I know how to refinish it. I mean, I have a vision. I was looking out at the river yesterday, and when the sun went behind a cloud the water turned this steely grey colour ...”

“Oh, that would be really pretty with the light walls in your bedroom.”

“And all the light that comes in from the windows?”

“And you could have some bright colours in your pillows ...”

“Or in the quilt.”

Meg smiles. “I can picture it.”

“I can too. For the first time. Which, I think, is a good sign.”

Meg nods. “Absolutely. It’s a great sign. And I don’t think you have to know why it happened. Back to ‘ours not to reason why’ – just accept it and go with it.”

“For Rand’s sake I hope it lasts.”

“And Rand would want it to last for your sake.”

In front of them a man holds the door to the general store open. “After you.”

The woman behind the counter – Maureen – glances up at them. “Betsy said you girls would be by. I have our entire inventory of Oreos in this box, and I packed a few other things she asked for in that second box.”

Meg reaches out to grab the nearest box, when Austen clears her throat. “Actually ...”

“Yes? Something you need?” Maureen asks.

“I’m going to buy a lottery ticket,” Austen says.

"What type dear?"

"I don't know. I've never bought one before. I guess one where you see if you've won or lost right away."

"An instant card, then." The woman pulls the rack out from under its protective cover and points to a row. "These ones are popular."

"Sure. Great. I'll take one."

"Most people choose their own, dear."

"Oh! Um, Meg, you choose."

Meg grins and reaches past the baskets overflowing with bags of sour gummies, and licorice, and Gobstoppers, and Ring Pops, to pluck out a lottery card for Austen. "I put all my good luck for today into picking this one."

Meg watches as Maureen hands Austen a nickel and points to where she needs to scratch the card.

Meg's phone pings with a text from Betsy, **All good?** and she's just thumbing, **On our way** when Austen squeals, "I won!" She holds the ticket out. "At least, I think I won. Maybe I'm wrong. I'm not sure how this works ..."

Maureen's takes the ticket. "You're not wrong, dear." She flutters both hands in the air and her cheeks go pink. "Not only did you win, but this is the largest payout we've ever had at this store."

"I did? I mean, I thought I did, but I couldn't believe it." Austen turns to Meg. "When everything started feeling so right this morning I told Rand I should buy a lottery ticket ... I just ... whoa ... this is ..."

"Your lucky day?" Meg looks at the ticket, then at Maureen whose whole face is flushed now. "Is that how much I think it is?"

"If you think it's enough to buy a nearly new Audi TT Roadster, then you'd be right."

Meg lifts one eyebrow. "That's oddly specific."

Maureen nods. "It's my dream car."

Austen jumps up and down, does a twirl. "Ladies! Ladies! I think we can all agree it's a *lot* of money."

"That it is." Meg puts her arm around Austen's shoulders and gives them a tight squeeze. "So, what are you going to do with all that money?"

Slate

SLATE BLINKS against the sun's rays beaming into her eyes. She hadn't noticed the sun lowering in the sky. Hadn't realized how long she'd been sitting here at the table cluttered with her phone, Alanna's laptop, a glass of water she meant to drink hours ago, and sheets of paper covered with the doodles she always scribbles while on hold.

She's made progress. Her phone – and now Alanna's laptop – are full of photos of splintered wood, twisted metal, blown-in branches.

There's a running catalogue of everything that was in the barn when it collapsed. As Alanna and her husband remember more things, Slate adds them to the list.

She has either original receipts, or itemized and signed entries for everything – lumber, building materials, and even coffee and pastries – that came onto the site today.

There are sticky notes all over a copy of Alanna's insurance policy with Slate's neat hand-writing pointing out relevant clauses.

Slate's even saved screenshots of the original tornado warning, and an Environment Canada tweet from this morning confirming the tornado touchdown.

She's worked with Alanna to fill out a proof of loss form, and has emailed a photograph of it to her contact at the insurance company, a woman named Violet. The two of them have spent long enough on the phone that Slate knows Violet has a tabby cat named Muffin, and Violet knows Slate has just lost her job at the legal clinic. "That was God's work you were doing, my love," Violet tells her. "When our family first moved to Canada a legal aid lawyer kept us from being evicted from our apartment. Good deeds are always rewarded."

"It's very kind of you to say so."

"Not kind at all. Truth. The world needs people like you, and your good work will come back to help you."

When Slate's on a mission like she's been today for Alanna, she becomes so focused that she doesn't notice hunger, or thirst, or weariness. But the accumulation of the stress of losing her job, the emotional upheaval of falling for her best friend's ex, trying to fall asleep during a major storm, then waking up to find that storm was worse than they ever could have imagined, has worn her out.

A yawn creeps up on her and she recognizes it too late to suppress it.

"Now, you listen to me." Slate smiles. She'd like to meet Violet in person. To see if she looks as definite as she sounds. Violet continues, "Your friend is very, very lucky to have you on her side. You've got this claim off to a great start. You've accomplished more today than most people do in the first week. I'll be sending an adjuster out from our Kingston office first thing Monday morning ..."

"Um," Slate begins, but Violet interrupts. "Yes, dear. I remember about the ferry. I'm sending him the schedule. Since there's nothing more you can do right now, I'm going to say good-bye to you and tell you to go sit down with some friends and have something to eat. Is there somewhere you can do that?"

Slate thinks of how that was supposed to be happening tonight. She checks the time. Yup. Right about now, under normal circumstances, she'd be in her bridesmaid's dress. Or, maybe not. Depending on the success of her shopping trip with Meg she might be wearing jeans with Meg wearing her dress.

Either way, she'd be standing by her friend's side. Listening to her vows. Not being able to hold in her smiles, or a few tears. Then, yes, sitting down with friends to eat.

Slate nods. "Yes. I can do that." Not in the way anyone expected, but she can do it. Then, suddenly worried that Violet will hang up, that there's something important she's forgotten, that she'll let Alanna down, she adds, "You've entered my number as a contact on the file, right? You'll let me know if there's anything more I need to do?"

Violet laughs. "As soon as your friend told me you were her representative, I put the number in the file. I'm telling you; you've done everything you can ..."

Slate inhales, ready to protest.

"... but I'll contact you if anything at all comes up."

"Thank you, Violet. I'm glad you were working today. Say hi to Muffin for me."

"It was a pleasure helping you and your friend, Slate. Now off you go for some food."

***

Slate couldn't be much closer to the food. She's sitting on the back stairs at the hall with a pile of corn by her left foot, shucking corn husks into a paper bag by her right foot.

Through the open kitchen door she can follow the conversations of the people – mostly women – inside. First there are two older women having a passive-aggressive discussion about pies. "Did you make this strawberry pie, Mildred? I admire you for trying – if it's not done right, strawberry pie can be sickly sweet." "Yes, well, that's not something you have to worry about with your rhubarb pie is it Angelica? The last time I had rhubarb pie it was so sour it peeled a layer of skin off my tongue ..." There's a pregnant pause before she adds, "Of course, I'm not suggesting that would ever happen with your pie."

Next, Slate recognizes Betsy and Meg's mom's voices as they roll utensils into napkins. "It's kind of you to help, Emily," Betsy says. "It's bound to be a disappointment that the wedding isn't happening."

Meg's mom answers, "Of course I want Meg to be happy, but I'm hoping since the wedding has been put off, maybe I can persuade her to reconsider certain aspects of it."

"Like what?" Betsy asks. *Yeah, Betsy, good question: like what?* Slate thinks.

"Well, just as a small example, borrowed cutlery rolled in paper napkins."

"You're right," Betsy says. "That is a small example."

Slate pushes the back of her arm hard against her mouth to keep from laughing out loud.

It's quiet for a few minutes. Slate slows down – she's nearly done with the corn, but after the problem-solving, and talking, and organizing of today, it's nice to sit here in the shade, with the ever-present island breeze lifting her hair away from her face. She almost doesn't want to finish.

A new set of voices drifts to her. Young she guesses, from the giggling. Giggle, giggle "... incredibly hot."

"Right? My mom would say he's too old for me, but ..."

"... all the more reason to go after him!" Giggle, giggle.

Slate's phone buzzes, so she misses the next couple of words. She unlocks the screen just in time to hear. "... only in town for a few days."

She's intrigued now, by both the message on her screen, and the hot, out-of-town subject of the girls' giggling.

The message is a quick read, but Slate will have to think about it later. **Slate, honey. It's your new friend Violet. You may know our company is headquartered in Halifax. Head office is partnering with one of the universities there to fund a free legal clinic. The woman in charge of the project is a long-time friend of mine. Just sayin' if you have a copy of your resume available ...**

The girls' chit-chat on the other hand ...

"Do you even know his name?"

"Better than that, I found him online – look, he's a journalist in Nova Scotia."

"Ooh, he looks even hotter in that photo. I'm totally going to hit on him tonight."

"Um, no. I found his photo. I get first dibs."

"We'll see. Not if I get there first."

Rather than making Slate think, it makes her feel. A rush of emotion, all at once. *Adam.* The girls are right about how hot he is. And his journalistic work is impressive. But her sudden clarity isn't about those things. It's about the thought of letting him go. Slip away. Meet somebody else. Go back home without them ever having a chance.

If she actually believes persistence is one of her best qualities, she'd better start using it.

And as for Meg and Adam's past – well, she and Meg can talk it through.

It's time to put myself first, Slate thinks. *It's time to go after what I want.*

She gets up from the steps, carries the shucked corn into the kitchen, then walks out into main part of the hall, where the chairs that were in rows this morning are now arranged around long folding tables.

She's going to find out where Adam is. She's going to borrow a car, or a bicycle, or a horse to get to wherever he is and talk to him. She's going to do this – she's not going to let anything stop her.

Right in front of her stand Meg and Jared and a man she's never seen before. The man turns to her and he's wearing a clerical collar. Then Meg looks at her and says, "Oh, Slate! Reverend Jim says we can still get married today."

Slate looks at her friend, and says, "If that's what you want, I'm here for you." She swallows hard. "I'm not going anywhere."

Lacey

Lacey wishes she'd left with Austen. Rand told them both they could probably be of more use at the hall than out here, but since Lacey still hadn't been able to find Fitch, she'd decided to stick around.

Now she's here with no Meg, no Austen, no Fitch, and no work. It's almost impossible to believe based on what it looked like when they arrived, but the area around the barn and, in fact, the entire property, is free of debris.

There are people consulting, and there are people unloading materials, and organizing them, and there are even people beginning to frame up walls, still lying flat on the ground.

There's not much work for a horse girl with a broom, though.

She takes one more turn around the barn area. No Fitch. She sticks her head into the house. No sign of him inside. She asks what's left of the coffee-and-snacks brigade and they shake their heads.

Her heart gives an extra *kerr-thump*. Her fists ball. Her jaw clenches.

"Are you OK?" one of the women asks.

She rolls her shoulders back. "Yes. Fine. I'm just ..."

Angry.

Yes, she is. Nobody else needs to know that, but it's the truth.

And it drives her to action.

On her way across the property to the station wagon she runs into Alanna. Lacey hands her the broom. "It was great to see you again," she says. "I'm heading out. If you see Fitch, please tell him I took the car."

Then she takes the car.

* * *

Heading to barn to check on Salem. Will hay horses, bring boarders in, etc. Anything else you want me to do?

Lacey texts Meg from the side of the highway about a kilometre outside of the village. She didn't want to pause back at Alanna's. She was afraid she'd reconsider. Afraid Fitch might suddenly show up and stop her.

She doesn't want to be stopped right now. She wants to go to Meg's barn and see her horse.

On the way through the village, she cruises by Meg's car parked halfway between the pub and the general store. She doesn't even slow down. Meg will get her text.

By the time she pulls up at the barn there's a reply. **Thanks for doing the barn chores Lace! It's a huge help. Nothing special for you to do – just the usual.**

As she's reading it another message buzzes in. **Make sure you get back here in time for the dinner. It wouldn't be the same without you!**

Something twists in Lacey's gut. Not the same without her. But things are going to happen without her. Tonight's dinner will happen, with or without her, and the life of this island, and the people who live on it, will keep going even while she's a time zone away.

Well, if she wants to change that, it's up to her to drive it.

She steps out of the car and takes a deep breath of summer air with, somewhere in the distance, the scent of fresh-cut hay, and right up close, the smells of sun-warmed earth, and horse.

Time to get stuck in.

Lacey readies the stalls of Meg's boarders who come in overnight, and brings the sweet mares in, hanging their halters on the big hooks outside their stalls and attaching their bell boots to the saddle pad bar on the stall door.

She refills all the hay feeders and checks the water troughs for the horses on turn-out.

She sweeps the barn floor clean.

Then she sits on the fence of Salem's paddock as the sun takes on that late-afternoon golden hue which, whatever other people say, is only this golden, and this warm, and able to set up this ache in her chest, here on this island.

Salem stands in the dead centre, right in front of the feeder, with Hops to her right, leaning in to grab a mouthful of hay, chewing it from his spot half a step behind the mare, then grabbing another.

Ever so gradually Salem takes tiny sideways-shuffling steps until Hops is completely crowded out on the right.

He good-naturedly backs a few steps, walks around to the mare's left and the whole procedure begins again.

Lacey shakes her head. "You sure know how to get what you want." She meant it about Salem, but she realizes it applies to Hops as well, just in a different way. Salem's subtle, but firm. Hops is flexible and persistent.

She hasn't been subtle, firm, flexible, persistent, or anything else in pursuit of her desire to stay here. She's just been silently hopeful, leading to her current mix of resentment and frustration.

That hasn't worked.

It's probably time to talk to Fitch.

She sighs, but she knows it's true.

If nothing changes, nothing will change.

And driving away from Fitch in a fit of pique just because her day didn't go the way she wanted it to is definitely not going to drive the kind of change she's looking for.

She watches Hops gather his courage and, instead of switching sides again, stand his ground – not budging his much-bigger body when Salem sidesteps into him.

"Alright. Here goes." She pulls her phone out and gets as far as thumbing, **Where are you ...** when a hum of tires grabs her attention and she lifts her face to see Jared's truck driving along the highway, slowing, and pulling into the driveway.

Except it's not Jared at the wheel.

It's Fitch.

She bites the inside of her lip and resolves to be firm, subtle, flexible, persistent and anything else it takes – most importantly to talk to Fitch and also to listen.

"Wish me luck!" she calls out to the two horses.

Meg

Meg's filled the pouch of a dusty apron with rolled up cutlery and is moving along the tables, getting them ready for the dinner to be served shortly.

Betsy helped her unfurl butcher paper over the folding tables pushed end-to-end to make long rows. Just as she had thought it would, the durable paper tied the mismatched tables together and there was a moment when she stood back and looked at it and felt a little stab to her heart.

"It looks lovely, dear," Betsy said.

Meg sniffed, "I know."

Betsy put her arm around Meg's waist and pulled her tight and said, "Just think – you've proven the doubters wrong – butcher's paper is wedding material."

Meg laughed at that, especially when her mom appeared from the kitchen just as Betsy finished saying it. "Oh! Well, that does look much better."

Meg straightened her shoulders. "Yes. It's perfect. And we ordered far more than we needed so there's lots left for the wedding."

Meg's mother blinked a couple of times. "If that's the way you decide to go."

"Good point mom. We also considered burlap. But this looks so good, I think we'll stick with it."

Her mom had handed her the cutlery rolls, and since then Meg's fallen into a rhythm, making it a game. Emptying her apron pouch, feeling it getting lighter. Thinking of each place she sets as a thank you for hard work given today.

The hall is filling with the scents of the massive pans of lasagna warming in the ovens, and last she saw her dad, and Carl, and a couple of other men were holding beers standing around the barbecue.

Every now and then a thought intrudes – This wasn't what you expected – then she thinks, Yeah, well Alanna didn't expect her barn to blow in, either – and that keeps her moving forward, picking out a roll, arranging the folded side down, laying it down straight just to the left of the chair, then on to the next one.

A couple of pre-teen girls come in with mason jars full of wildflowers and set them at regular intervals along the tables. She smiles, "Those look pretty!" and the one girl nods, "I'm going to be a celebrity floral designer when I grow up." She snaps a photo and Meg figures it'll soon be on her Insta floral arrangement page.

Her phone buzzes with a text from Jared – **You all good?**. She hasn't seen him much today, but he's been checking in regularly. She appreciates both the space and the support. It's a balance that works for them. It's why they'll be fine. It's why this delay is just a tiny hitch in the rollout of the rest of their lives.

She snaps a photo of the neat, simple tables made graceful by the flowers **Perfect dry run.**

He writes back, **I like your attitude (and the tables!). I'm on my way there now.**

"Well, this looks wonderful!"

Meg whirls around to face the minister. "Hello, Reverend. How nice that you could make it."

"Well, I'm not in the habit of missing wedding ceremonies."

"Oh …" Meg takes in his linen suit and the sky-blue shirt he's wearing with his clerical collar – it's what he wore last month when Meg – along with most of the island – attended the wedding of the island's postmistress to the decades-long owner of the garage. His marrying uniform.

"I ... that is, with the tornado, we ..." she hasn't had to say it out loud to anybody yet – their announcement at Alanna's farm was about tonight's dinner here. Everyone knew what it meant, but she didn't have to say, "This means the wedding is off."

Now though, with Reverend Jim in his marrying suit in front of her ... she takes a deep breath. "Jared and I assumed the wedding couldn't happen today." That's a softer way of saying it.

"Well, I assumed it would." The minister blinks and stays quiet in that way he has that's sometimes calming, sometimes unnerving.

The joy Meg feels when Jared walks in the door isn't just because she's happy to see him. It's also because she doesn't have to face Reverend Jim alone.

"Jared!" She turns to Reverend Jim. "Here's Jared!" – stating the obvious – something she always does when she's off-balance. "Reverend Jim came over to perform the ceremony."

"Oh!" Jared says. "We assumed ..."

Meg shakes her head, and Jared stops. "Reverend Jim assumed we'd go ahead."

Then Slate walks in and Meg turns to her, "Reverend Jim says we can still get married today."

"So, what are you going to do?" Slate asks.

Meg meets her best friend's gaze, then keeps turning. Locks eyes with Betsy, arms laden with the dreaded paper napkins, then with Austen, clutching a big bin of crayons that often comes out to entertain children during parties and meetings.

She pauses for a minute, trying to read her mother's expression, then thinks better of it. This isn't her mother's decision to make.

She scans the rest of the room. Plain, yes. Sparse, definitely. Also, bright. Simple. Homey. Perfect.

She wouldn't want to get married anywhere else.

Her eyes land on Jared.

She wouldn't want to get married to anybody else.

She thinks of what she said to Austen earlier – how she was adopting an "ours not to reason why" mindset – except now she doesn't have to. Now she has the chance to decide for herself what she wants.

She knows what she wants.

The smile starts with her heart and takes over her face, lifting the corners of her mouth, her cheeks, and her spirit.

He's smiling the same way, right back at her.

She steps across to him, hands out, and he takes them in his.

"What are we going to do?" she asks him.

He pulls her close and wraps his arms around her and says, "We're going to do the exact thing we were always meant to be doing today."

"Well! Thank goodness for that!" Betsy's voice echoes in the otherwise-quiet hall. "Somebody get that girl a clean apron!"

CHAPTER TWENTY-SEVEN

Austen

IT'S SO MUCH MONEY.

On Slate's orders, Austen's picking through the overgrown verge between the hall parking lot and the woodlot behind it, cutting wildflowers that are probably weeds, but will look pretty in bouquets.

It is a lot of money, and it isn't. Like Maureen said, it's not even enough to buy a brand-new luxury car. It wouldn't make much of a dent in the price of a house these days. But for people like Alanna hit hard by the tornado – it could really help. And for Rand, who works tirelessly with the tools he has, when he could definitely use newer ones, it's a windfall. And for her ... well, it's funny how all of a sudden the inspiration is flooding in. It's not that the things Austen wants are big or extravagant – some paint and good brushes for furniture refinishing, rubber matting in Mac's new shelter – it's that knowing she can pay for them herself changes everything.

She spies a cluster of purple-speckled white blooms and leans in to gather them. They release a minty smell. A breeze ruffles her hair. A shaft of sun hits her hand.

She's filled with joy, delight, and purpose, too.

There's no denying the money helps. It's as though the universe took the way she felt this morning and said, *"Don't slow down – keep moving."* The universe, or the province's Lottery and Gaming Corporation – it doesn't matter which – *ours not to reason why.*

"Oh good."

Austen whirls around at the sound of Slate's voice. Her cheeks hurt from smiling. "It is good," she says.

Slate pauses. Tilts her head to the side. "Are you OK?"

"Literally could not be better."

Slate holds out her hands for the flowers Austen's collected. "Well, I'm so glad to hear that, because I have another job for you."

***

Austen's on her way back to the general store.

"Ring pops," Slate told her.

"Excuse me?"

"Meg says they have Ring Pops at the general store – she noticed them earlier – since their rings are still in Kingston, pick one up for each of them."

"What flavours?"

Slate looked at her like she was crazy, but to Austen it feels important – if Meg can't have her real ring she should at least have the flavour of edible ring she wants. "Forget it," she said, when it became clear Slate wasn't going to answer. "I'll decide."

Now she's on her way to the general store to choose rings for Meg and Jared – no pressure – then she's supposed to go on to the house. "My bag's there," Slate said. "There's a dress I was going to wear for the ceremony. If you bring that Meg can wear it. It'll be a bit short on her but with her legs she can carry it off. Oh, and I think she might have a strapless bra from prom – might as well bring that so no straps show."

As Austen was heading out the door thinking, "*Ring Pops, dress, strapless bra ...*" Slate called, "Oh, and Austen?"

"Yes?"

"Be quick, OK? They want to do the ceremony in less than an hour."

Austen's driving thinking, "*Ring Pops, dress, strapless bra, quickly ...*" Every now and then she remembers the money she won. It's true what they say about money – it can't buy you everything. It can't buy her out of this rush to get … *Ring Pops, dress, strapless bra, quickly.*

It is nice, though. Such a relief. To be able to help that nice Alanna Turlington and to be able to take the financial pressure off Rand. The burden he's shouldered so completely while she's been unable to focus enough to move forward in her work – to contribute financially. All that will change now. They have breathing room now.

Oh! Whoops! She's driven right by the store. She pulls over to park then hurries back. *Ring Pops, dress …*

Inside, Maureen laughs. "Back for another lottery ticket?"

"No!" Austen's panting. "Ring Pops please! Two!"

"Oh-kay …" Maureen furrows her brow. "What flavour?"

"See?" Austen says. "It's a perfectly reasonable question!" She closes her eyes and scoops two out of the basket. Looks at them. Wrinkles her nose. "Watermelon!" She drops them back and grabs two others. "Blue Raspberry – perfect!"

She slides a five-dollar bill across the counter and turns to run back out the door – "Keep the change!"

Now she just has to get … *"Dress, strapless bra …"*

"Oh! Austen!" Austen slows to a halt in front of Jared's mother.

"You're here! We thought you were stuck in the city. Because of the ferry."

Mrs. Strickland shakes her head. "I texted Jared that I was able to get a ride over on a private boat, and he said to come ahead and bring my dress." She laughs. "Which I did, but I'm a bit weighed down with the pies I baked and everything else I had to bring."

Austen looks at the woman holding a garment bag, a cooler, and a couple of miscellaneous bags. "I have my car. I'd offer you a drive to the hall, but I have to go out to Meg and Jared's first. Still, you can put your things in the car so you don't have to carry them."

"That would be lovely, Austen. The walk to the hall is short enough when you're not carrying a cooler."

"Great. I'm parked right here." Austen opens the door and leans in. "If you just hand me your garment bag … oh!"

"What is it?"

"I don't need to go back to Meg and Jared's after all!"

CHAPTER TWENTY-EIGHT

Lacey

"SHE LOOKS HAPPY," Fitch juts his chin toward Salem as Lacey climbs into the truck.

Lacey knows it's nice that he actually cares about her horse. She knows Fitch wouldn't be the person she loves if he didn't.

But today she wants him to ask how she is instead.

"Why wouldn't she be? She gets to stay right here. At her home. Where she's happiest." Lacey concentrates on doing up her seatbelt. She doesn't meet Fitch's eyes.

"Is there something you want to talk about?"

"Maybe there was earlier today, but I couldn't find you anywhere and the day's gone from bad to worse, so right now – no, there's nothing I want to talk about."

Fitch shrugs. "OK." He puts the truck in drive.

Lacey wants to know where he was all afternoon. She wants to know why he's driving Jared's truck. She wants to know where they're heading.

But she really hates herself right now.

She's sulky and grumpy and self-indulgent. What she's feeling may be legitimate – homesickness is, right? – but she's incapable of expressing it in a rational way right now.

Add in the fact that she agreed, in what seemed like a reasonable and adult way at the time, to live in Nova Scotia with Fitch – to have a setup where neither of them would have home court advantage – and any complaints she makes now will just sound petty and pathetic.

She stays quiet. Stares out the window at fields full of beef cattle, then one where a draft horse foal frolics with his mother.

They pass a row of bee hives – she'd like to keep bees at their family's farm. She'd like to do so many things – she'd like to help with the crops her dad and Jared already grow, but she'd like to diversify as well.

Keep bees, sure. Maybe talk to Alanna about alpacas. Look into new crops, like hops. Even consider specialized farming – cut flowers, for example.

Not all at once, of course, and not without research and planning, but she'd like the chance to research and plan.

She sighs.

Fitch shoots her a look, then fixes his eyes back on the road.

She knows what he's asking, even without him asking it – *"are you ready to talk yet?"*

She shakes her head.

They roll through the village and past the hall with it's parking lot now nearly full.

Aren't we going to dinner at the hall?

She wants to ask but the silence has taken on a life of its own. She can't break it now.

They keep driving, up the little hill that marks the end of the village, then down the swooping curve where all summer the road is shade-dappled by the overhanging trees.

At ten years old she remembers walking home this way with two of her cousins, licking ice creams they bought in the village, their flip-flops sticking to the rubber-melting asphalt of the highway. Except here, in the shade. They always walked more slowly here.

The truck passes a series of unspoiled, clapboard summer cottages.

They used to wait until the cottagers went home Sunday night, before sneaking up to the windows, peering in. Seeing who left the places tidy, and who was a mess. They'd sit on the lawn chairs, giggling at their own audacity, wondering what it would be like to only be here on weekends. Lacey, for one, never wanted to find out.

Now they cruise past the turnoff to the old quarry. The driveway of Lacey's best friend growing up was right across the highway from the quarry turnoff. Sometime since they were kids, municipal numbers have been put up on all the houses. Stark white font on a green background. Reflective. Now, Lacey supposes, people might use the address – "It's 40357, Highway 98" – but back then it was all reference points. "The Old Quarry," "The Ellicott Ferry turnoff" "The Drummond place."

Fitch wouldn't know that. It's not his fault, but now, as they approach her driveway, he slows because he sees that number sign staked next to the mailbox. Not because they've drawn even with the tree that was hit by lightning in the big storm on her thirteenth birthday.

He takes the graveled driveway slowly and coasts to a stop outside the empty house.

He doesn't say anything.

The silence holds so much power she's not even sure she has the strength to break it.

She sighs. Fidgets. The truck engine ticks. A breeze rustles the leaves of her favourite tree – the huge aspen that shades her bedroom. It's obvious the dog is still out with her dad by the bravery of the fox that peeks his face out of the long grasses by the lawn.

Someone's got to talk. And Fitch has learned from the very few fall-outs they've had – he won't speak up first.

Lacey wrinkles her nose, purses her lips, then breaks the silence. "Why are we here?"

Fitch drums his fingers on the steering wheel. "Two reasons."

She's not in the mood for guessing games. It takes all her restraint to keep her tone reasonable as she asks, "Which are?"

"Well, one is for you to get changed for the wedding."

"The ... excuse me ... what?" More guessing games, but the glimmer of hope she's feeling takes the edge off her annoyance.

"The wedding's on."

"The wedding's on? Meg and Jared's wedding? But I thought ..."

"Apparently the minister showed up, ready to perform the ceremony, and Jared's mom got a lift over, and they figured the meal was going ahead anyway, with most of the people who were going to be guests, so why not?"

"Why not?" Lacey breathes it.

"If you could make it, of course," Fitch says. "Which is when I said I'd get you and deliver you in time for the ceremony."

"Oh!" Lacey snaps to attention. "I'd better run. Get changed. I don't want to hold things up."

Fitch reaches over and lays his hand on her arm. "You have time."

She lifts her eyebrows.

"OK, not a ton of time, but long enough."

"Long enough for what?" Because now Lacey's thinking about the earrings she was going to wear with her dress and whether she knows where they are, and also, how the dress has a tie that looks much better if it's done up in the back, and she wonders if Fitch could do that for her …

"Long enough to talk about here."

Suddenly Lacey's not thinking about any of those things anymore. "Here?"

"You being able to work here, on the farm – to help your dad. To use what you learned at agricultural college on your family's property."

Of course, it's exactly what she wants – she couldn't have put it better herself – but …

"But," she says. "How? I mean, we agreed, neutral territory. I went along with it. I even see why it was a good idea." She pauses, then adds, "I just didn't know how hard it would be."

"Well, now," Fitch says. "Neutral. There's a word. What is neutral?"

"Are you really asking? Like, do you want a dictionary definition?"

Fitch rubs his temples. "This island is not neutral. You can never actually be an islander if you weren't born here. And I wasn't born here."

"Also, everyone knows just about everything about everybody else at all times – not neutral."

"Agreed. Not neutral." Lacey narrows her eyes. "I'm not sure what you're saying."

"Kingston could be neutral."

Lacey freezes. Holds her breath. There it is – hanging in front of her – a compromise. An offer. A solution. Too good to be true. Too much in her favour for her to just reach out and take it. "But I went to high school there."

Self-sabotage, or honesty? She doesn't know, but she had to say it.

"Did you like it?"

"Did I like what?"

"High school."

She wrinkles her nose. "Of course not. In my experience, only truly spirited and involved people love high school, along with a few others who are so terrible they make high school miserable for everybody else – and I was neither of those two."

Fitch laughs. "Well, I think you're lovely just the way you are. The point is you didn't enjoy your time in Kingston. You don't have roots there. We could put down roots together."

"There are some really great neighbourhoods ..."

"Somewhere close to the ferry, so you can get back and forth easily ..."

There's a bubble of excitement rising in Lacey's chest. This could work. This could be amazing. High school unhappiness aside, Kingston is a great city. Character-filled houses and streets, easy access to water, lot of amazing restaurants. Such an obvious solution for them.

She shakes her head, because Halifax has all those things, too. And if this was such an obvious solution, why has it never come up before? "Why?" she asks Fitch.

"Why what?"

"Why now? Why Kingston? Why would this be an OK move?"

He blushes. It's something she's almost never witnessed. Fitch is straightforward. Fitch is honest. Fitch is ... unbelievably hot when he blushes.

She leans in and kisses him and he makes a noise that could be surprise, then pushes back against her lips and runs his hand up the back of her head, fanning his fingers through her hair.

Mmm ... why do Meg and Jared have to be getting married? Why can't she and Fitch just sit here in the glow of the late afternoon sun and kiss and kiss, until they decide to maybe go inside, or even ... her eyes slide to the backseat, and Fitch pulls back. "No way. Not in your cousin's truck."

She sighs. "I know." Then remembers what started all this. "Why were you blushing?"

He presses a hand to his flushed cheek. "Well, I'm thinking now it might be for a different reason than two minutes ago."

"Fitch ..."

"Fine," he says. "I'm actually happy to tell you because if that's what I got just for blushing, I'm definitely going to get lucky when I tell you this."

"Tell me what, Fitch?"

"I applied to grad school."

"Aarrgghh ... I know you applied to grad school. You told me Professor Kumar recommended that you apply to work in his lab."

Fitch nods. "He did – that's true – but Professor Hinshaw also recommended that I apply to work with her thesis supervisor."

"Oh-kay ... I'm sorry Fitch, but I have no idea what this has to do with anything, and my cousin's getting married any minute now, and I'm wearing work boots and a baseball cap."

Fitch takes her hand and squeezes it until she stops talking and looks him in the eye. "I'm listening," she says.

"I got hired by Professor Hinshaw's thesis supervisor."

"That's great."

"To work on a really cool research project."

"Amazing."

"In a state-of-the-art lab – they just finished building it last month."

"I'm really glad for you, Fitch ..."

"At Queen's."

"That's ... *what*? Where?"

Fitch nods again. "You heard me. In fact, one of the other grad students who works in the lab was at the alpaca farm today. I was talking to him for ages about the school, and the department, and Kingston ..."

"That's why I couldn't find you."

He nods. "Yeah. Sorry I was MIA. Was it for a good enough reason?"

Lacey cocks her head to the side. "I think maybe it could have been."

"You think so, huh? What do you think about the whole idea?"

Lacey shakes her head. "I think it's a lot to think about ..." She looks at the clock on the dash. "And I think I'd better get changed!"

Fitch bites his lip. "You're right. I get it – it's a lot to take in all at once."

Instead of opening the truck door, though, Lacey leans back to him, nuzzles her nose in under his ear, nibbles at his neck, and says, "What I feel, though, is excited."

"Mmm ..." Fitch says. "That makes two of us."

CHAPTER TWENTY-NINE

Meg

HER FRIENDS take care of everything.

No clean apron needed – Austen runs in with a dress, folded carefully in a padded envelope, somehow trying to explain that the dress was Eliot's. Meg unfolds it. Thinks it's something she'd never have chosen in a million years. Tries it on and is transformed.

She wouldn't have chosen it because it's different from anything else she'd normally wear, and she suddenly sees that's right – it's good to feel different. Plus there's the whole Austen / Eliot vibe making her very happy.

The dress is taken care of, and so are the rings, with Austen handing her mom two Ring Pops.

Meg holds her breath as her mother looks down at the two extremely plastic, eye-poppingly-coloured, oversized candies. Her mother inhales deeply and, behind her, Meg hears Betsy doing the same thing. Then her mom smiles and says, "Blue Raspberry. Great choice, Austen," and Meg thinks she might never have loved her mother more.

Then Austen says, "Guess who I picked up ..." at the same time as Jared's mom walks through the door closely followed by Lacey, in a swish of long hair, swirling skirt, and sparkling earrings. "Auntie Jane!" Lacey calls, and hugs her aunt. "You're here!"

"You're here," Meg repeats, mostly to herself. Then, a little louder. "You're here ... you're all here ... Lacey, you look beautiful, and Austen, thank you for everything, and Slate – well, I couldn't do this without you here, and Betsy was part of this story from the beginning, and our parents, well we know nobody wants what's best for us more than you do, and Fitch and Rand you're both such good sports for doing anything and everything we need you to, and Reverend Jim, thanks for kicking our butts into gear, and Jared ..." she pauses. "Jared, are you ready?"

"I'm ready if you're ready."

"I'm ready."

***

A glow of late-afternoon sunlight washing in the windows backlights Jared as he stands across from Meg, and holds her hand, and says, "When the ferry's running and when it's not."

Meg laughs. "Through heat waves and tornados."

"In barn clothes, or an apron, or a borrowed dress," Jared winks at Austen who gives a little bow.

Suddenly there's the sound of guests' feet shuffling, followed by the sharp tapping of hooves and a yelp, "My bad! Totally on me!" and the tiny goat appears at Meg and Jared's feet and lets out a sharp bleat.

"With goats!" Meg shakes her head. "Even with goats."

Cam scoops the goat up and swoops him away and the people standing closest to him hear him whisper, "Everything's better with goats."

"With everybody we love around us," Jared adds.

Meg nods. "The only way I'd ever want to do this."

Reverend Jim clears his throat and says, "With the blessing of everyone present here today, I now pronounce you legally wed. I invite you to seal your promise with a kiss."

Even though Meg appreciates Reverend Jim's more egalitarian presentation of the option to kiss (instead of the good old, "You may now kiss the bride,") this part of the ceremony still makes Meg cringe a little inside.

It's not that she doesn't want to kiss Jared – she very much wants to – but she doesn't want to have to hold back, or to stop.

She wants him to kiss her, and her to kiss him back, and him to take this dress off – it really is a sweet dress, but it hugs her ribs awfully tightly – and at that point she doesn't want other people watching.

So when the door at the end of the hall flings open and a man's voice yells "Slate! We need to talk!" and Adam steps inside before taking in the group on the stage and saying, "Oh, whoa! Sorry, my bad!" Meg doesn't really mind.

In fact, the instant flame in her normally cool-as-a-cucumber best friend's cheeks makes her laugh out loud and, instead of kissing Jared, she turns to Slate and kisses her very pink cheek.

Then Jared opens his arms and kisses his mom, and all around them people are kissing each other – Carl's kissing Betsy on the forehead, and both Austen and Rand, and Lacey and Fitch are kissing as though they're the ones who've just been given permission by Reverend Jim.

Even Cam's cradling the pygmy goat in his arms and kissing the top of its hard little head.

Now Jared's by Meg's side and twining his fingers through hers and whispering, "OK?" and she's saying, "Perfect, actually," and she finds that on second thought she doesn't mind kissing Jared here in public after all.

Slate

SLATE'S EYELIDS feel like they're closing over sandpaper. Her cheeks hurt from smiling and smiling – mostly genuinely – how can she not smile when Austen stands up and tells everybody she's donating the cash Alanna and her husband need to replace their old, uninsured truck.

Or, when Meg and Jared dance their wedding dance to a pretty melody played by Betsy on the old piano on the stage with Carl accompanying on the guitar.

She smiles as she listens to Lacey and Fitch planning their move back:

Lacey: "I told my dad I'd be back in time for the plowing match."

Fitch: "That guy from the lab I was talking to today put me in touch with a friend of his who just finished renovating an apartment in his basement."

Lacey: "We'll have to find a subletter for our place in Halifax."

Slate tears up a bit when Alanna stands on the stage and thanks everyone for all the work they've done all day, from clearing the site to securing the alpacas, to running the coffee-and-baking table, "... and to Meg and Jared for sharing their special day and this amazing meal, and to Slate who, from what I can tell is an insurance whisperer."

A rise and fall of laughter ripples through the room and somebody squeezes Slate's shoulder. Hope balloons in her as she whips around – she thought she'd see Adam as soon as the ceremony was over, but she hasn't caught sight of him since – but it's Meg.

"Oh," Meg says. "I'm not who you wanted to see."

Slate forces a laugh which quickly turns genuine, and rises to her feet. "Of course you're who I wanted to see. Only the most privileged people get a one-on-one with the bride on her wedding day."

"Well, this bride would consider it a privilege if you'd take her out for some fresh air." Meg waves her hand in front of her face. "It's getting hot in here!"

Slate links her arm through Meg's. "I know just the spot."

In the kitchen two older ladies chat as they wash and dry dishes. They glance toward the girls and Slate puts her finger to her lips, "Don't tell anyone I'm sneaking the bride out for a few minutes."

She and Meg settle on the steps.

There's nothing vaster than the island sky, and nothing prettier than when it's laced with star spray like it is now. The lawn behind the hall, and the bush that surrounds it, are alive with cricket song. Slate takes it all in with a long look, a roll of her shoulders, and a deep breath, then lets out a long sigh. "Wow, thanks for coming to find me. I didn't realize how much I needed the fresh air."

"It's been a big day."

Slate nods. "Sure has. I can't believe everything that's happened. As if a tornado and a wedding weren't enough. Austen winning the lottery. Lacey moving back home. Makes me wonder what's next."

"Well," Meg says. "For me it's this." She holds out her phone and Slate peers at the screen displaying a message from Cam's partner, Lynsey. **Congratulations Meg! Also, sorry Meg! I didn't know Cam had taken the goat until he'd left … probably because I'd previously told him a goat is NOT** a suitable wedding gift. I'm sorry I wasn't able to join him, but I wonder if you and Jared would come here for a mini-honeymoon? I've just put the finishing touches on our first rental cabin and you'd be doing me a favour if you could test it out for me (It's on the other side of our little lake, which means a good distance from Cam and all our goats). Let me know if you can come and I'll make sure everything's perfect in the cabin.

Slate scrolls through the pictures Lynsey's sent, then looks at Meg. "You're going, right?"

Meg sighs. "We thought of going somewhere later in the fall. After the soy's harvested. That would give me time to organize somebody to look after the horses."

"Meg, it wasn't a question. That cabin is amazing. You're going." Before Meg can protest, she continues, "And, I'm sorry, but you have someone to take care of the horses right here, right now. I'd love to know who you think would do a better job than me."

"But don't you have to leave?"

"I can stay for the next couple of days."

"Hmm ..." Meg says. "Tell me your 'what's next,' and we'll see about that."

"Here." It's Slate's turn to hold out her phone, open to the message from Violet.

Meg reads it then raises her eyebrows. "Halifax?"

"I know. It's crazy, right? It's too much. I mean ..."

"You mean you just met Adam and you have a big crush on him, and now you've been offered the perfect job in the city where he lives."

"Right. Exactly. There's no way I can take it."

"Slate ..."

"Yes?"

"Would you take this job if it was in Fredericton? Or Winnipeg? Or Kingston?"

Slate snorts. "Are you crazy? I'd take this job pretty much anywhere. I mean, maybe not Toronto, because I'd have to live in a cardboard shack on a legal aid salary in Toronto but, yeah, it sounds like the perfect job for me."

"So, you have a crack at the perfect job for you, in an amazing city, and someone you could really like also happens to live there. I'm not seeing the problem."

"It's too easy. It's too much. He'll think I'm following him."

Meg shakes her head. "No. Your parents would think you were following him."

The truth of the statement hits Slate right in her chest. "You know me too well. You're absolutely right. It takes me right back to my university applications when I was head over heels for Jeev Prasad and he went to U of T and my mom and dad told me there was no way I was 'following a boy' to school and they wouldn't let me apply there."

"They were wrong then, and if they say anything like that they'll be wrong now."

It's Slate's turn to shake her head. "They won't see it that way."

"It's not their life. Besides, why would you even tell them about Adam? Whatever does or doesn't happen between you two is your business."

"I'll still know. I'll still feel it."

Meg squeezes Slate's arm. "Listen. It's not a question. You're applying for the job and if I were you I'd mention to Lacey and Fitch that you might know somebody who wants to sublet their apartment." Meg pauses, then says, "Slate, why not be happy?"

Those words. They remind Slate of what she always loved about her legal aid work. How powerful it is to find the perfect words to change somebody's mind. *Why not be happy?* Slate leans in and presses her forehead to Meg's. "OK. I'll do it for you." She pauses, then adds. "I'd do anything for you, which is why I have to ask ..."

Meg interrupts her. "Please don't. I just married the perfect person for me. I definitely do not care if you date somebody I once dated very briefly years ago. In fact ..."

"In fact, what?"

Somewhere in the cricket-filled darkness a throat clears. Meg switches on her phone flashlight and shines it on Adam. "In fact, I texted Adam to come and keep you company so I can get back to my new husband."

Slate's stomach does a long, slow flip-flop driven by nerves, and excitement, and hope.

Meg leans in and gives her a kiss on the cheek – "See you later, bestie" – then she's gone in a swirl of white dress and a flutter of her fingers through the inky night air.

"Hey," Adam says, "Can I sit down?"

Slate takes another deep breath. "There's nothing I'd like more."

"Really?"

"Definitely."

"Because earlier …"

Slate angles toward him. Her knees bump up against his and she doesn't pull them back. "It's been quite a day, Adam. Quite a few days, actually. I'm not exactly myself, and I'm not entirely sure what I'm doing, but I'm completely sure I want to be sitting here with you right now."

There's a shifting noise and suddenly the entire length of Adam's thigh is pressed along hers and she realizes it's a bit chilly out here, and he's lovely and warm. "Why don't you tell me about it?" he says.

"I'd love to. Inside. Where it's warm. But while we're out here, I think I'd prefer it if …" she leans in and finds his lips with hers. They're soft, and perfect, and –

yes – warm. She'd normally close her eyes about now, but tonight she leaves them open and while tiny star bursts explode inside her from the headiness of having Adam rest one hand on her hip and crook his fingers over her waistband, and put his other hand on her cheek to pull her in tight while he kisses her, she watches the burst left by a meteor shower in the sky.

She's not worrying about her job, or whether she'll move to Halifax, or what might happen with Adam tomorrow, or the day after. She's thinking, *Why not be happy?*

Meg

THE LACING on Hops' back glows delicate and ghostly in the light of the near-full moon in tonight's clear sky.

There's nothing delicate or mysterious about the gelding himself, though. When Meg and Jared lean on the fence next to the paddock gate he shakes his long neck, lets out a low whicker, and begins a loose-limbed meander in their direction.

When Meg calls, "Hey handsome," his ears flick forward and he increases his pace to a quick walk, then a cruising jog until he reaches them. He comes to a stop, head outstretched, nose finding Meg's hand, heaving a deep sigh as she cups his muzzle.

"This one will be hard to let go of," she tells Jared.

"He definitely has personality."

"He has everything." She turns her head to Jared even as she continues to stroke the velvety skin around the gelding's nose. "I've been afraid to say this out loud, but he reminds me of Major."

"Why were you afraid?"

She shrugs. "At first I guess it was because maybe I thought he wouldn't live up to it."

"And once he had?"

She gives a hollow laugh. "Well, I lost Major, didn't I?"

"Right." Jared says. "Well. You don't have to lose this one."

Meg pauses, mid-stroke. The gelding pushes against her fingers. "What do you mean?"

"I called the barn in Kingston. They gave me his owner's number. I made her an offer. She accepted."

"You ... what? So, you bought him?"

Jared laughs. "Conditional on you wanting him, I've bought him. I'm supposed to call her tomorrow. Which also answers 'why.' He's your wedding gift. I told her I'd call after the wedding – after I checked with you."

Meg can't speak. Can hardly breathe. Has to fight an overwhelming urge to clamber between the fence rails and throw her arms around the big horse.

On second thought ...

She snugs her dress tight around her thigh and steps through the rails.

"Where are you going?" Jared asks.

Hops stands still, and when she reaches her arms around his neck he sighs. She changes her mind. He's not exactly like Major. Major always had a slight aloofness to him. It was something Meg loved about Major, because it was part of him, but she also adores Hops' through-and-through affection. "Come on." She hopes Jared can hear her voice muffled by a solid thousand pounds of horse.

He does. She knows it when his arms encircle her, and they lean into the big gelding together.

"Thank you," she whispers.

"To be honest, there was no way I could let him go," Jared says. "He meets me at the gate every morning. I'm pretty fond of him."

"I'm pretty fond of you."

"Are you?" he says. "So, what's my wedding gift then?"

Meg giggles. "I left it at the house."

"You did?"

"I did."

"Can we go get it?"

Meg turns into him, feels the long-known leanness of his body against hers, his hands that always settle in just the right place in the small of her back, his lips brushing her forehead that are so ridiculously soft on somebody with such work-calloused hands and feet. "Oh yes. Let's go."

***

Meg never sees the bow wave of the ferry, without feeling at least a twinge of excitement. It's anticipation that the boat's close enough to be able to see the white water frothing in front of it.

That and the motion, the power of the huge vessel, plowing through whatever weather it encounters, 365 days a year.

She loves it here, but it's exciting to be in line behind Cam's truck, heading over to Kingston to finally pick up their rings, then hit the highway for a couple of days away from everything in the little cabin Lynsey has ready for them.

They'll be gone just long enough to make Meg be excited to come back.

The ferry docks, and the island-bound cars roll past. The brake lights of the vehicles ahead of them flare as engines ignite in preparation for boarding the boat.

"You good?" Jared asks her.

She flashes her Ring Pop at him. "I'm good."

He laughs. "We can eat those after we get our real rings."

She's wondering whether she could bring herself to do that, when a whinny rises above the background noises of the idling truck engine and the summer breeze.

Meg looks up to the ridge where she stood with Hops such a short time ago and there they are: Lacey and Salem, Austen and Mac, and Slate on Hops.

Those women. Those horses. This place. Her life.

Tears threaten and she tries to blink them back, then thinks, why? Why not cry when it's for all the right reasons.

She gives in to the ache in her chest, lets the tears spill and roll down her cheeks, and turns to Jared.

He reaches out, swipes a tear from her cheek, and says, "I know. I know. And it's only going to get better from here."

PLEASE LEAVE A REVIEW!

REVIEWS help me sell books. More sales let me write more books. A simple star rating and a few quick words are all that's needed to help other readers decide if they want to read my books.

To review, please follow this link – https://tinyurl.com/ReviewRW – or, use this QR code:

IF YOU LIKED THIS BOOK …

… you might enjoy Tudor's other books. Read the first chapter of *Objects in Mirror*, Book One in the Stonegate series, to find out.

Chapter One

THE WHIPPER-IN calls my number – "Seventy-two, you're on deck!" – and, as though he understands that's us, Sprite dances sideways, nearly slamming the clipboard-wielding gentleman into the white fence boards.

This is the big class of the day. I'm as excited as Sprite, but one of us has to stay calm. Serenity doesn't come naturally to hepped-up off-the-track thoroughbreds like Sprite. Which leaves me to be the sensible one.

I sink my heels deeper in my stirrups, settle my seat more firmly into the saddle, and point my thumbs up.

Back straight, big smile, look cool, and send Sprite, in his beautiful sweeping trot, into the ring.

Where he promptly grabs the bit, yanks his head down, and lets his back heels fly.

Sprite wants to jump. Sprite sees no need to bend or flex; to circle or warm up. He enters the ring with his eyes and ears flicking from jump to jump.

In Sprite's mind, all I'm good for is pointing him at the first obstacle, after which I should back off and stop bugging him so he can finish the course.

I've ridden horses that can autopilot courses. Some of my competitors own horses like that. Sprite, however, is not one of those horses. Given his head, Sprite would jump everything twice, then get bored and jump the fence out of the ring, to keep on running and jumping everything in his path.

I know this because I've seen him do it.

So I give him a firm half-halt as I smile wider than ever, mutter "bugger" under my breath, and step him into the forward canter we need for our approach to the first fence.

He clears it by eighteen inches, and jump two, as well. He leaves at least two feet between his belly and the top rail of jump three and throws in a tail flourish on the landing. *Here we go.*

Sure enough, as he rounds the far corner, Sprite throws out a lightning-fast series of bucks. There are always three in quick succession, and those trademark three bucks will leave me only four or five precious strides to set him up for the diagonal combination.

"Excuse me!" I use my seat and my legs and my hands and my voice, too – a horse like Sprite requires every aid in the box – and we battle our way over the three increasingly wide jumps. By the end of the line, he's flying, reaching, digging, and the sturdy white ring fence is coming faster and faster, and we need to turn the corner in enough control to get over the tall vertical propped on the short end.

"Listen!" I tell him, but it's a tool for me too, reminding me first and foremost to get it done. Forget pretty, forget elegant; those can come later if we make the flat phase but for now, my priorities are (1) don't knock down any jumps, (2) don't die.

We dig in deep to the base of the vertical and, with a super-athletic effort, Sprite twists himself over it without bringing the rail down. To celebrate, he indulges in his biggest buck yet.

Despite all the noise and activity of the show grounds, all I can hear is my own voice ordering Sprite to "Smarten up!" then Drew's yelling, "Go, girl!"

"Go!" I tell Sprite. *Go, go, go*, and, with that, we're not fighting any more. We're four jumps from being home and we want the same thing – to get over them fast and clean – I lean forward, give Sprite a nudge, and soften my hands.

The new gear he clicks into is so fast it's almost scary. I hardly have time to breathe, as Sprite pins his ears against his neck, throws all his energy forward, and jumps the jumps.

When he's not in mid-air, he's running flat-out, and when he clears the last jump, I have to keep him galloping around the ring because there's no way I can stop him in time for a polite exit from the gate.

Fantastic, amazing, exhilarating, unbelievable. I'm hooked, hooked, hooked. Want to go right back in and do it again. Want to jump like that all summer long.

"Pinch me!" I tell Drew as I ride out of the ring, because I can't believe Sprite's mine for the season and I *do* get to do this all summer long.

"Don't relax yet," Drew tells me. "You're through to the flat. Now you've got to make him behave."

***

Four days later, my Sprite-induced jumping high hasn't worn off. It doesn't hurt that we placed third; an amazing showing, considering Sprite had to suffer through the flat portion of the class.

It's not like school's been distracting me. With the temperature hitting twenty-eight by fourth period, even the teachers are more focused on beaches and cottages than learning objectives and curriculum.

When I get on the school bus for my final ride of the year, and settle my butt onto the ripped vinyl of my usual seat, I have nothing left to think about – nothing to plan for, study for, or worry about – other than riding, and showing, and Sprite. I drift into a play-by-play rerun of our weekend jumping round so vivid that half my brain's still back at the show grounds as I step off the bus at the end of our gravel country driveway.

Only to be rugby-tackled around the knees.

"Ooof!" I yell. My arms flail for something, anything, to break my fall. Finding nothing, I go down hard, hitting the ground with a thump, swiftly followed by the second thump of my backpack full of books, bouncing off the gravel to hit me on the head.

"I'm Sowwy, Gwacie!" It's Jamie, my three-year-old brother, straddling my waist.

"I might believe you if you didn't look so happy," I tell him.

"Come on, you; give Grace some peace." Annabelle says, hauling him off, then holding out her hand to help me up. "He's so excited to see you. He can't stop talking about how you're going to be around all summer long."

Jamie runs off ahead of us, weaving from side to side across the driveway, stopping every now and then to make a wild jump in the air or kick out at his shadow. He reminds me of Sprite but without the bad nature.

"He insisted we make lemonade for you." Annabelle's trying, just that little bit too hard, to keep her voice light and easy. How can one simple sentence be so loaded, mean so much more than the sum of its words?

"Good," I say. "I'm hot." And Annabelle smiles. I've said the right thing: *I'll have some*, just not in so many words.

She takes my hand and, even though I'm nearly sixteen and, even though she's my stepmom, I let her. Even squeeze back a bit and, actually, it feels quite nice.

If you liked the beginning of Objects in Mirror, why not read the rest of the book? Objects in Mirror is available as an eBook or paperback on Amazon. This QR code will take you to it!

ABOUT THE AUTHOR

TUDOR ROBINS is the author of books that move your heart, mind, and pulse.

A little piece of Tudor's own heart is in many places: the central-Ottawa neighborhood where she lives, the Gatineau hills and Eastern Ontario countryside where she loves to hike, Wolfe Island and the St. Lawrence River where she loves swimming and paddleboarding, and the university towns that are currently home to her children.

When she's not writing, Tudor rides, runs, quilts, and walks with her best friends and her Jack Russell / Potcake mix, Cara.

Please contact Tudor at tudorrobins@gmail.com!